Red Horses

Donna Lynch

RAW DOG
SCREAMING
PRESS

Published by Raw Dog Screaming Press

Bowie, MD

First Edition

Book design: Jennifer Barnes

Cover: Steven Archer

Printed in the United States of America

ISBN 978-1-935738-38-1

Library of Congress Control Number: 2013935108

www.RawDogScreaming.com

Red Horses

Thanks, Kristina –
much love!

x ♡ x

Dedication

For Rebecca

Acknowledgements

Many thanks to Jennifer Barnes and John Edward Lawson (RDSP), Faryn Black, Clovis, my wonderful family, friends, and EL fans, and most of all—my husband, Steven.

London, 1887

To strangers passing by on the streets, to her professors, classmates and acquaintances, Anastacia Millerovo would have seemed a normal young lady: courteous and learned, ribbons in her hair, all the usual appendages in their proper places. But she was not a *usual* girl; Ana was not made of such frivolous things as fairy dust and paper dolls, but of things much darker. She was born of Russian winters and the deep waters of the Black Sea. Beneath her skin, she was the colour of volcanic sunsets in Martinique and her dark hair smelled of the marketplace in Algiers. Her thoughts came in myriad languages and voices, though when she spoke, her voice was only one exhausted composite. Her heart beat like the drums of African slaves, and she was sewn together with the absolute best and worst pieces of her deceased mother and father. She was worn like a tattered shroud by countless ghosts.

Ana could hear the thoughts of those around her, the living and the dead, which made her privy to others' secrets and intentions, and at times she was nearly deafened by the cacophonous voices of ghosts and murderers, priests and *loa* and a vast assortment of entities she could only presume to be demons, all of whom drove her mad with their ravings. She learned throughout the years how to silence some of the more trivial and mundane thoughts of man, but it brought little relief as Ana would never know what it was to be alone, in silence and peace. Anastacia Millerovo was a carrier of souls, or what the people of Martinique called a *cheval*. It was a title that some wore with pride, but for Ana it meant only exhaustion and torment. She had seen this part of herself in dreams many times; her bloodied, skinless body draped in white veils, empty and cavernous beneath her bones and her own delicate head replaced with that of a grotesque, scarlet, wild-eyed horse. She would have you know this so you remember that you cannot trust your eyes, for they are vicious liars. They will tell you she is a normal girl, when truly she is a monster.

But Ana lived with this day after day, and so it was since her mother's murder. She was five years old then, and it was one of the first genuine memories she had.

⤚⤙

Official word of her father's death came on a Friday, though she'd known it in her bones at the very moment of his passing. The news arrived in a very cordial letter courtesy of his attorney, a man who signed his name Allen Grace, Esquire.

She met with Mister Grace the following Tuesday to discuss her predestined future. The estate of Vladimir Millerovo came with a number of clauses, and this came as a bit of surprise to her as the articles indicated that her father had not forgotten her in his madness. Truthfully, it came as a surprise that there was an estate left at all. She presumed he'd drunk their fortune away while she was at school.

In an elegant office, the benevolent Mister Grace carefully explained the terms of her father's last will and testament. Ana was to inherit a generous sum of money, a large plot of land in Lancashire and much to her astonishment, a husband—the son of her father's accountant, and the nephew of the attorney that sat before her—a young architect called Nicholas Grace. If she agreed, Nicholas would build a home on the land, and she imagined it was her father's design that they would live happily ever after, although he'd left no article in his will instructing her how to forget the terrors of her childhood.

She knew nothing of this Nicholas person other than his profession, and those of his father and uncle. What had gone through her father's mind that led him to arrange a marriage? They were neither nobility, nor she some peasant girl to be bartered away with a dowry. She was horrified at the very idea. Why, after *everything*, would her father have done this to her? Of course, after everything, why should she be at all surprised?

Despite her preternatural abilities, her father had always been difficult to understand. His mind had been cluttered and poisoned for as long as she could remember, and now the chaotic recess of her brain that had been reserved for him was silent and would remain so until his ghost might decide to torture her further with vivid images and enigmatic messages from beyond, the way her mother had done since her death. Ana meant no offense to her mother's spirit; she knew she wished only for her story to be told with honesty and accuracy, but it was still so very painful to hear her mother's distinct voice day after day for years after she so violently left the world.

Ana sat quietly in Mister Grace's spacious office thinking first about her mother's voice and carrying in her bag the clay jar that was left for her after her mother's murder. Then she stared intently at the attorney's face and tried to imagine him stripped of twenty years' worth of wear. He was handsome enough for an older fellow, though she never cared too much for the company of gentlemen, nor had she ever given much thought to their appearances. The other girls at school would steal away from the nuns at every opportunity and whisper about *this darling boy* or some *fine-looking lad* from St. Andrew's. They'd swoon over piercing eyes and swirls of thick, shimmering hair, but she did not join them. Those foolish girls knew nothing of the suffering love could bring. They had never seen love fall sick under the weight of jealousy and bloody rage.

As she prepared to leave, Grace handed her a heavy envelope. He told her in a gentle voice that it was a journal written for her by her father, something she knew the moment she held it in her hands.

"I am sorry for your loss, Miss Millerovo. And if I may be so bold…we *will* be family soon, so if I can do anything for you, please just ask."

She forced a smile, feeling that she could have been more gracious. For possibly the first time in her life she stood in the presence of someone who did not have a scandalous secret or monstrous intention at the forefront of his mind. The only thoughts she could hear mirrored his words, all of which were laced delicately with sympathy and concern.

The Journal of Vladimir Millerovo to Anastacia Millerovo

To ~
Anastacia Millerovo
Care of Mr William Grace/ Mr Allen Grace, Esq.

September, 1886
London, England

My Darling Ana,

I will presume I have retained the right to call you mine ~if not in spirit, then in flesh and blood.

I am not the man I once was, so please forgive my languid prose, as well as my atrocious penmanship. It is the best I can manage anymore, and to-day has been a good day. My apologies in advance for the pages drafted on the bad days. None the less, I feel it is my duty as your father to write these words. After I have taken so much, this journal is the last useful thing I will ever be able to give to you. Do with it what you will ~ burn it, use it to further curse my already damned soul, bury it in the ground ~ but please, please read it first and know that every last word, beautiful or terrible, is true.

If you are at all like your mother, and I'm certain that in so many ways you are, then you must be thinking, 'Why is this miserable specimen of a man wasting my time with his drunken ramblings?', and I shall tell you why. In a brief moment of sobriety, it occurred to me that you, in your eighteenth year, are nearly a woman and you know so little about your beautiful mother Veda and our life together before the unpleasantness. And I cannot lie to you now, so I must say that I also wish to tell you about the man I was before things fell apart, before Martinique. I know in my gut that I will be dead soon, and I cannot fathom taking this knowledge into the fire with me, when it rightfully belongs to you.

~

The pounding against the door caused Vladimir to jump, and he watched helplessly as black ink spilled onto the wooden table and dotted the pages of the journal.

"I thought I told you to go away, you foul bastard, and take your vulgar fetish with you!" Vladimir called out in response to the startling interruption. This was the second time today.

"Aw, come now, Mille'ovo. You don' mean that. She's just downstairs and this'll be your final chance to have a turn at 'er till next Tuesday, you realize!" A rasping, jagged voice yelled from the hall. "She even got hair as black as raven feathers, just the way you like 'em!"

Vladimir slammed the book shut and rushed to the door, toppling his rickety chair in the process.

"*Christ*, man!" The pale-skinned man stumbled across the threshold as Vladimir nearly tore the door from its hinges. "You tryin' to break my bloody neck?"

"*The way I like them*? What do you presume to know about my tastes, Pinkney?"

The tall Russian caught the man by the arm and hoisted him upright with little effort. He reminded Vladimir of a laboratory rat, with his pointy nose, crooked little mouth and dishevelled white hair. Pinkney could have easily been mistaken for an albino, if not for his green eyes.

11

"I *presume* to know," Pinkney said with a sneer, "that you like your morsels delivered young and fresh and dark-haired. That's what you'd request any other time!"

Vladimir released the man with a shove and backed away; satisfied by the thud that sounded when Pinkney hit the wall.

"I may prefer my women young, Pinkney, but I am not interested in that pitiful child you've been peddling all week. How old is she anyway…eleven, perhaps twelve?"

"What do you wan' me to do? My customers like to break 'em in. Not ever'body's interested in damaged goods the way you are, Mister Mille'ovo."

"You are a child molester, Pinkney, and you should be repulsed by your own reflection. Now get out of my sight before you ruin my mood and prevent me from finishing my work for the day."

"Your work?" Pinkney chuckled. "What sort of work are you able to do anymore?"

"I'm writing, if you must know."

"*Writing*? Oh, yeah…tha's right. You used to be one of them intellec'tuls, back before you drank yourself useless, eh," the pale man laughed. "So what're you writin' with those shaky hands? A book about how to be a failure?"

"If that were my venture I'd have certainly called upon you for my research, but as it is, I'm writing something… for my daughter."

"You got a daugh'er? Imagine that." The man smiled. At least three of his teeth were missing. "Well, all right then. I'll let you get about your business. But I got just one question before I go."

"What?

"About how old is she?"

"Get out before I kill you, Pinkney, and don't even *attempt* to conjure an image of my child in your revolting little mind."

"Well, I'd hate to see you have yet another dead body to your name, so I'll bid you good day, my dear Mister Mille'ovo!"

12

This was not how Vladimir had hoped to begin his work. He wanted nothing more than for his beautiful Anastacia to read the words of a clear-headed man, so she could fully understand her history. He'd sworn to himself that he would only write in the journal when he was sober to insure this, but with distractions such as Pinkney surfacing at every turn, his faith and his self-control seemed to wane yet again, just the way it had shortly before Ana was born. Really, the way it had his whole miserable life.

I've gone through this in my head again and again, where shall I begin? Shall I begin from to-day and take you back through the years or shall I spare you, for the time being, from the tales of my despondent days and nights, my misanthropic adventures with opiates and prostitutes, (I promised you the truth) and begin at your beginning? Since I am having a good day, I think I'll tell you of a time, despite its trials, that brings a smile to my haggard face. It begins in October ~the bitter month that masquerades as Moscow's autumn~ only months before you were born.

Moscow, 1868

Moscow is cold and Veda is pregnant. Vladimir remembered spending the better part of each passing hour repeating this sentence silently until it became an involuntary action. He'd done this until his mind scrambled the words, sometimes leaving Veda cold and Moscow pregnant. He had never been this obsessive when he was drinking. When he was drinking, his thoughts never stayed in one place long enough to create a problem, but such was the price of sobriety. *My wife and child are worth any cost,* he thought in earnest, and spent many more hours trying to convince himself that he wasn't trying to convince himself of it.

What no one understood at the time was how tremendously difficult it was for Millerovo to work under the conditions afforded to him. No one, not even Veda, knew how competitive his field had become. He could hardly make her understand, she cared so little for science. Veda believed in deities, she believed in omens and ghosts and devils. She believed in things like fate and miracles. She had no mind for things like physics and chemistry and modern medicine, no mind for reality and concrete fact, nor would she be able to comprehend that no matter how much time or effort he spent, no matter how much research completed or how many articles written, there would always, *always* be some other scientist who gave more, discovering the one component that Millerovo missed. Always some other *doctor* to publish an article that would inevitably be held against his own as an addendum with the sole purpose of highlighting, then superseding, all of the points, *his* obsolescent points, to which he'd dedicated and sacrificed so much time. Things were rapidly and forever changing, and with each new discovery came another thick, wet blanket of pressure for Millerovo to wrap around his shoulders.

Vladimir remembered walking down the street, numb to the bitter October winds, while the words in his head went like this: *Moscow is cold and Veda is pregnant and our room is not warm enough to see her through to a healthy delivery and I could figure this out if I had a moment's reprieve from these thoughts and I could think clearly if I could only...* He'd paused on the corner, rubbing his already raw face and tired eyes. *It's been twenty-three days since I had a drink.* The day he found out that Veda was with child, he promised her no more, but twenty-three days later—*twenty-three days*—he was left with nothing but an upset stomach, trembling hands, and a hundred impossible questions. *How am I supposed to figure anything out like this? What does she want from me? How am I to resolve this and never allow myself one moment's reprieve?*

"What do you want me to do, Veda?" he muttered to himself as the wind slapped him repeatedly in the face.

I want you to give me a miracle, Vladimir. I just want you to give me everything you have. That's all, my love... he answered silently. *Just everything.*

That was the year that Vladimir Millerovo first became aware that he would most likely never redeem himself—not to his wife, not to anyone. He would always be a weak-willed disappointment to his family, and whenever he'd arrive at a crossroads, he would invariably choose the path of greatest complication and resistance. Happiness, like religion, was an unattainable ruse designed for the ignorant, and suddenly he could find very few reasons to go home.

⤛

It was the thought of you, my little pet, on that dreadful day ~you who did not yet have a face or a name~ that led me home. You, my brilliant star, were the beacon on that dark, filthy street, and for all of the misery and despair that my presence later wrought upon you and your mother, I think that I could not have resisted your sweet, silent call even if I'd tried.

⤛

The dark, narrow stairwell of the tenement he and Veda had lived in during their time in Moscow would have reeked of terrible human odour had it been warmer. As it was, the semi-conscious vagrant that usually obstructed the only passageway to the stairs hardly ever bothered Vladimir. It was too cold for the man to stink and he was thin enough for Vladimir to step over with little effort. The chemist had enough on his mind as it was (there would have been no one to complain to anyway; the landlord was a faceless entity that assumed all complaints to be requests for a new, and most likely inferior, residence) and the vagrant was there every day, so at least Millerovo's piss-poor situation was, if nothing else, consistent.

In the doorway of the miniature room at the top of the stairs, Vladimir, well over six feet tall, removed his hat, bowed his head and entered. And this was how his wife would first see him each evening: head hung low, shoulders lurched forward in shame. How he despised this life he'd given her, and now a self-fulfilling prophecy all because of decisions made by architects a half a head shorter than he. Everything in that city was designed for small people; just one more reason for Vladimir to feel like an outcast.

He never truly needed to concern himself with Veda's opinion of his sullen entrance. She would be seated at the dirty little window, staring out at the dirtier street below, and she never turned around as the door creaked or as her husband would mumble a quick greeting. She never looked upon him in judgement.

"And how is our luck today?" she said to the window, pulling her shawl closer to her slender body. The draft of the stairwell had come in with Vladimir.

"As good as yesterday, my darling."

Veda chuckled softly, far down in her throat. It was the same deep place from which she always spoke; that wonderfully dark, velvety canyon inside an olive-hued swan neck. She never lowered her head for anyone or anything. Vladimir often studied her neck, impressed by its great length and slope, entranced by the arrow-shaped columns of silky black hair that adorned it. He enjoyed it the most when he could see those delicate hairs; when the rest of it was wound up at the top of her head, all plaits and twists, like a crown of magpie feathers. He adored the little spiralling hairs that spilled over her ears and onto her cheeks and the longer wisps that collided with her dense eyelashes. She was a strik-ing woman, too beautiful to be contained in the frigid and decrepit box they called home. And now, another beautiful creature held within her body would be condemned to serve time in the box as well.

"Look, Vladimir…it's snowing," Veda's serene voice brought him out of his head and back into the room. Her voice had been a paradox at times, mingling the intonation of a sultry woman with that of an excited child.

"Just what we needed, eh?" he muttered, prodding the last of the embers in the stove.

"You act too old for a young man. Already worn and ragged at twenty-nine," she teased. "Anyway, I enjoy the snow. If my choice is to see the world stained in grey or blanketed in white, then I choose white."

Vladimir smiled at his young wife. He knew then as he knew now that he didn't deserve her, nor did she deserve to be blamed for his failures; why his career had withered and stagnated, why his research had been unable to make the slightest bit of difference in the world of medicine, why there were moments when he would have sold her and his unborn child into slavery for a drink. He hated himself for all of it. He hated himself then and now for smiling at his wife while he thought such dreadful things. When she smiled back, he wondered if she had any idea what a terrible man he was.

She did, of course, if not in exact words then in raw emotion. Veda knew many things about the way people felt, whether they spoke of it or not. This was an accepted trait in her family; both her mother and grandmother were blessed with intuition. One of her brothers—her twin, Luca—had the gift as well. The only male in the Romanian family to have any inclination toward such otherworldly abilities, Luca received much harassment from their older brothers Gregor and Alexi. For years, the two older siblings referred to Luca as their other "little sister."

It was a small price to pay for Luca. He and Veda shared a bond made of something that felt like lightning. They had secret languages and rituals, and they had entire conversations without speaking. They had hideouts in the rocky caves along the coast of their village. They had the sound of the sea hitting stone, and bright blue sparks that jumped between their hands when they touched their palms or fingertips together. Gregor and Alexi could tease all they wanted. They would never have what he and his twin sister had.

Their mother Lavinia and her mother—their grandmother—Iona kept close watch over the twins. The Sera family was a superstitious one and the matriarchs knew the potential that lay, for the most part dormant, in the children. They tried

17

to keep Veda and Luca's *gifts* hidden from their neighbours and clergy, but most of Constanta was just as superstitious so rumours were inevitable. Lavinia and Iona were often too busy keeping the older brothers from tormenting Luca to concern themselves with outsiders. Iona, though she loved her grandchildren, was not above threatening to curse the boys if they continued to bother the twins.

Life got easier for Luca when his brothers were old enough to go to the sea with their father Alexandru to fish. Alexandru Sera was a fisherman by trade, selling his catch each day to the town market. There was nothing spectacular about his occupation, his father had been a fisherman, his sons were becoming fishermen, his neighbour was a fisherman, and so on. It was a difficult market in these coastal towns, but growing cities meant more mouths to feed, so despite the competition there was business enough for most. Of course, some were luckier than others. Some had children with very special abilities, such as knowing from where the best catch would come each day or when storms were bound to strike.

The Sera women were weavers. Their flawless techniques were passed down to each new generation through the blood, it seemed. The cloths and garments they produced were known to be some of the finest on the coast. Young Luca would sit by quietly while Iona, Lavinia, and Veda spun. He listened while Iona would whisper chants, a word for each loop pulled taut. Lavinia would join in, then Veda, the way children sing in a round, and the room would fill with the melodic hum of chanting and spinning and whirring until he thought the whole place might tumble down. It never did, though one time the window shutters and the front door blew open simultaneously with such tremendous force that Veda instinctively jumped, dropped her spindle to the floor, and ran trembling to her brother.

When Vladimir brought her to Moscow, it became apparent that Veda, then in her twentieth year, was saddened that her *gifts* were no longer what they used to be. The reason was obvious; she and Luca had too much time and space between them. For most of their lives, they had believed that there could never be another person to come between them. In secret, neither saw the harm in refusing marriage and spending their lives together. What man or god could ever deny that there were two people so connected, each designed specifically for the other, that the laws of the church or the land couldn't be bypassed in order to preserve what some greater universal force intended? In fact, at that time, Romanian law stated that surnames were not legally required for any person or family, though if compelled to do so, citizens could choose any name they desired. Veda and Luca's family had voluntarily chosen Alexandru's deceased mother's first name, Sera, as their surname and Iona's late husband, Lavinia's father, had taken a variation of his father's name, Dumitrius, which he shortened to Dumitru. The twins reasoned that if necessary, they could flee to another city and take up residence there, under a new name. They agreed on *Estela*, for it was only from the stars that such a love could be created.

What the twins neglected to consider was that their unusual relationship, carefully guarded by their mother and grandmother, would also become subject to much scrutiny as time went on. Behaviours deemed normal and acceptable in children were not looked on so favourably by the mothers as signs of adulthood surfaced. Iona chided the twins for sitting too close to one another or for always touching. Lavinia questioned Veda and Luca ferociously with harsh whispers, so Gregor and Alexi did not hear, whenever they were away from the house for long periods of time. Luca would often receive a sharp slap in the face if one of the mothers caught him staring at his sister, and so it was for Veda as well.

By 1866—Veda and Luca turned eighteen that year—Lavinia and Iona feared the worst and finally revealed their concerns to Alexandru. There was no hiding it from the older brothers anymore, either. The three men remained very calm as Lavinia spoke. Gregor and Alexi had become mirror images of their father, not only in appearance, but in demeanour as well. They had become good men. Having grown out of their once insatiable need to torture Luca, the brothers kept an emotional distance at first. Veda and Luca were like strangers to them now. To have relations with a cousin, the brothers agreed, was one thing, but this—if it was true—was something completely foreign to them. This—if it was true—seemed very wrong.

It didn't take Alexandru long to decide on a course of action. He loved his children and saw no benefit in humiliating them or possibly crushing them under false accusations, so made no mention of the situation to the twins. Instead, one clear, warm day he walked into town to find his only daughter a husband, preferably one that would take her just far enough away from Luca to save their souls.

⤳

The day her father went into the city to look for a husband for Veda was the day that she and Luca stole away to a shore cave and committed the one act that their family had feared the most. While they lay on the gravel and sand floor of the cavern, entwined in each other's limbs, bright blue sparks jumping from her naked stomach to his thigh, their father Alexandru was introducing himself to a pale young Russian called Vladimir Millerovo.

Alexandru, usually a collected man, was not thinking all too clearly that day. He ran what he was about to do through his head again and again on his way into town. *I am about to find a man to marry my daughter. A man, he could be a good man, to take my child away from our family. I am doing this for her, for my son, for my family. It is the moral thing to do*…but as Alexandru walked along the dusty, winding road he knew deep inside that really, he was about to find a stranger who could be evil just as easily as he could be good, and he was about to hand to this stranger his only daughter. He hoped his children would forgive him. He hoped it was God's good hand guiding him down this path, and not the hand of his own fear.

⤳

"He's going to take you away," Luca whispered in the darkness.

Veda nodded and nuzzled closer to his chest. Of course they knew what would happen upon their father's return.

Luca was shaking at the idea. "We should just go. We should leave now and find our home somewhere else, away from here. We can be different people, we can…"

Veda hushed him. "Luca, *no*. Do you really want to fight this and tear our family apart? They have always loved us and been good to us. Our father works so hard and our mother and grandmother teach us many things. Our brothers are good men. We cannot do this to them."

"Veda…please say you will not go with another man."

"Do you really think any man or any distance will make me stop loving you? We will never be without one another. It's impossible. Take comfort in the knowledge that you have what should have been my husband's."

Luca held her tightly and exhaled hard to keep from weeping. Veda worried for him. She had seen this coming for some time. Why hadn't Luca?

"I saw it," he replied aloud to her silent wondering. "I just didn't want it to be true."

Alexandru heard the stranger's voice from behind him. The sound of broken Romanian rose above the noise of the market, as the one voice out of tune rises above the harmonious choir. He turned to find the body that belonged to the strange dialect, a task that could only have been easier if the stranger had been riding upon Alexandru's back.

The man was very tall and thin and sullen. He was trying to purchase a hat, unsuccessfully haggling with the vendor, in part due to his choppy tongue. The vendor showed him no mercy, confusing the man and attempting to con him into a price that was higher than fair.

Alexandru shouldered his way past the oncoming mass, nearly thrusting himself into the stranger's torso. He knew the vendor and snapped his fingers very near the man's head, commanding attention. Both men jumped a bit, startled by Alexandru's abruptness. Alexandru eyed up the stranger, who in turn stared suspiciously at the dark, sturdy man. It was a terrible moment for him as he realized that he had no idea, really, what he was looking for; scars, defects, some certain immoral gleam in the eye or tension in his hands? This was insanity, that much Alexandru knew. What he should do now is turn and go home to his family and figure out something else, something less likely to make his beautiful Veda hate him.

"*Sera!*" The vendor barked at him, baffled first by the interruption, then by Alexandru's hesitation. "What's your business here? What's this…" he snapped his fingers spastically at Alexandru's face in a mocking gesture, "…about?"

The tall stranger waited nervously as the men argued in their quickest native tongue; accents far too thick for him to comprehend. He glanced down at his hands; they were shaking horribly. He suddenly felt sick, and considered running away. The sun was beating down upon him now, and he could feel the burn of heat and humiliation turning his brain to liquid. He thought he might faint. He didn't even notice as the vendor and the dark man's shouting subsided into normal speech.

The vendor turned back to the dissolving stranger and, with much visible displeasure, thrust the hat towards him. The stranger took it with great care and caution, as though it might bare its teeth and bite into his hand. He held out his coins with his other hand—it was the amount he'd initially offered—and the vendor snatched them up with bitter contempt and turned away, mumbling obvious curses at both men. Vulgarity always sounded the same, no matter the language, Vladimir thought.

He circled around to thank the man for his help, but Sera, stricken with a sudden change of heart, had already ducked into the crowd. The stranger impulsively darted through the mob after him and within seconds he was in reach and he cried out for the man to wait. Alexandru felt a hand grasp his shoulder and came to a halt.

"I wanted to…eh…to thank you," the stranger said in slow, lumbering Romanian. Despite his rudimentary delivery, he had an oddly pleasant voice. It was modest and deep and distant. He was slouching, bringing himself eye to eye with Alexandru.

Alexandru shook his head. "It's fine." He was careful to speak slowly and clearly. "That man is not to be trusted. He waits for people like you to come along and give him all of their money."

"People like me?"

"Strangers. You are not from here."

He looked at the ground bashfully and fidgeted with his hat. "No. I am from Moscow."

Sera watched the stranger shift and twitch. He seemed like a nice man, but something was wrong with his nerves. It could be nothing. *Or it could be something very bad,* he considered. "Why have you come to Constanta?"

The stranger kept his head down and grimaced. "Holiday," he muttered hastily. "I am on holiday." He raised his head and met Alexandru's eyes. "Is it always so warm?"

"Today, yes."

The awkward silence between them did nothing to calm either man's nerves. Alexandru knew why he, himself, was nervous. Here he was, after nearly escaping a potentially disastrous situation, right back on the path in which he started. He should have just kept going. So now there was no one to blame for the sinking feeling in his gut. But what about this tall man who hangs his head low and forces his shoulders to be forward? What reason did this man from Moscow have to be nervous? He wanted to know the story of this troubled-looking young stranger who used his new hat to cover his large, trembling hands.

The stranger cleared his throat with little success. His mouth was not much better than the dusty road they stood on. "I, eh…I am not used to the heat."

Alexandru nodded again. "What is your name, son?" *Son? What are you doing, Alex?*

"Millerovo. Well, Vladimir… that is to say…" he sighed deeply, painfully. "My name is Vladimir Millerovo…" His frustration was apparent as he slipped back into Russian on the incidental words.

Alexandru could see this was a man who lived a difficult life. Despite his size, Alexandru could easily picture the young man being washed away, right there in front of him, into the swarm of villagers and disappearing forever. He was little more than a shadow.

They waited quietly together for some time, neither could easily gauge how long, and in that time it became apparent it was no accident that they met. If you had asked either man then what it was that stirred within them, what unsettling familiarity washed over them as though they had seen this coming or possibly dreamed it long ago, it is doubtful that either could have qualified the feeling.

"Well, nothing is to come of any of it just standing here in the road, eh?" Alexandru knew it was an odd thing to say, but truly could think of no other reasonable suggestion. "Come with me. We will feed you, and I have just the thing to calm your nerves."

Millerovo nodded humbly, perspiration streaming down his rigid face. "It would be nice to be out of the sun," he said.

Alexandru suggested that he put on his new hat to keep the sun from his eyes and face and Millerovo blushed a little.

"Of course," he grinned nervously. "You know, I'm not certain as to why I even bought this hat. It's rather ugly, don't you think?" He smiled and placed the shapeless, brown wool cap on his head, haphazardly. He was dangerously close to light- heartednes—possibly light-headedness. He could not tell which.

Alexandru smiled back. "Yes. I didn't want to offend you, but yes, it is a very ugly hat."

As promised, Vladimir Millerovo was taken out of the hot sun and given food and drink. Enough drink, in fact, to numb him to the scrutiny of Alexandru's family. For the most part, the family had been cordial to the stranger, with the exceptions of Luca—who would not look him in the eye, nor speak directly to him—and Iona, who spent the better part of the meal with her sunken eyes fixed upon his own, flickering back and forth as though she were reading some urgent message. Alexandru's eldest sons were quiet, but Vladimir sensed that they were merely taking a cue from their father, holding back all inquiries until a more appropriate time. Lavinia, who knew the true reason for the stranger's presence, concealed her anxiety by humming quietly to herself as she served her family and the guest a feast, one large enough to imply that she'd been expecting company. It was a terribly uncomfortable dinner, each member of the party uncertain of the other's intentions, uncertain of who knew what, and why, exactly, there was a strange, nervous Russian at their table. But as Alexandru poured thick drink after drink for him, Vladimir found himself becoming less interested in the reactions of the Sera family, and more interested in the young woman next to him. He could smell her black hair. It smelled of sand and darkness.

There was no question in his mind that she was the most beautiful thing he'd ever seen and she was completely aware of this. She knew exactly what it was doing to him as she brushed against him with her arm and when she shifted in her seat and let her knee fall against his thigh under the table. She knew how it stirred him when she sucked the grease of the lamb from her fingers. This was no amateur that sat next to him. She knew how to weave herself into the minds of men as well as she could spin her thread. She also knew that when Vladimir sobered up, he would be terrified of her.

When she finally spoke, it set his hands to trembling again. "Vladimir Millerovo from Moscow," she said in a rich whisper. "What do you do in Moscow besides freeze half to death?"

Vladimir shoved his hands under the table. Her voice had a sobering effect on him and suddenly his nerves awoke and shot to the surface of his skin.

25

"I… I am a chemist. I, eh… just completed school and now I am trying to find work… and I am doing research."

Veda looked unimpressed by this. She was more interested in the goose flesh that covered him. Under the right circumstances he would be a very pretty man, although other than his height, there was nothing all that exceptional about him; brown hair and grey eyes, long, thin nose on a long, thin face. Sometimes it's only a matter of the slightest measurement that separates average from beautiful: the distance between the eyes, the length of the nose, the space around the mouth or the height of the cheekbones. Vladimir's spaces were set well, as though they'd been carefully calculated. He was so close to magnificence, but years of mistreatment and neglect chipped away at that brilliance, leaving only a painful reminder of what he could have been.

"A chemist," Alexandru said, proudly. "That is quite something. Your father must be very proud."

"I hope he is. It has been some time since I have seen my family."

"Well, if you were my son, I would be very proud."

At that, Luca groaned and left the table, whispering something Vladimir couldn't understand, though it was definitely seething. Now there was a splendid man. No one in the Sera family had been cheated out of beauty, but Luca and Veda had obviously received the wealth of it. They were the mirror image of each other, and both more stunning than anyone Vladimir could ever recall seeing. Lavinia called after her son as he kicked the wooden door open and rushed into the newly fallen darkness.

"Leave him be, Lavinia. He'll be fine," Alexandru said.

⤜

It seemed to be the thing to do that night, disappearing into the pitch black the way Luca had at supper. Vladimir was the next to go, after his stomach began to protest the copious amounts of liquor served to him. Though it most likely wasn't the liquor, he reasoned, but the addition of a generous slab of meat. It made little difference, as it was all given back to the ground moments after he left the house. When it was done, he stumbled blindly down a path that led to a stony beach. The new moon gave him no assistance in his journey and the alcohol that remained in his system was no help, either. He fell several times before resting at a collection of large rocks. He was by the sea now; he could hear the lapping of water against rock louder than his own thoughts. It sounded beautiful and painful, but from where Vladimir sat, all he could see was darkness. There was no horizon, no wave crest, no shimmering silver reflections, just a great black void. *That's what lay before me…a great black void.* Then he laughed.

His laughter echoed off the surrounding stones and for a moment he thought he might not be alone. "*Salut?*" he called out. Another echo. *What was the younger one's name?* "Luca? Is that you?" His own voice came back again, this time surprising him. It was strange to hear his voice reflected back to him in a foreign language. He was still thinking in Russian. He found it fascinating that no matter how many languages he learned to speak, he always thought in his native tongue. It was like some kind of gift, his understanding of languages. He learned them so quickly because he could understand how they worked. That was the way of everything in life. That was why science was so easy for him. Wasn't that all science was anyway? Understanding the process?

And Vladimir indeed understood process. There was very little he couldn't figure out how to do and yet, for some reason, Vladimir never seemed to excel in any one field. He had been a mediocre student and now he was a mediocre chemist looking for middling research for less than average pay. Vladimir spent so much of his time learning everything he could, that he afforded himself no time to ever master a particular skill. For the young scientist, it was a matter of quantity, not quality. This was his downfall. This was the reason he spoke Romanian, Dutch, German, French, Arabic, Chinese, Spanish, Italian, and English, but not exceptionally well.

One thing he'd mastered over the years, however, was drinking—heavily and often. He became a different person altogether when he drank, and frankly, he enjoyed that person much more than his sober self. Sober Vladimir was nervous, *always* nervous and shaking (so much that he didn't notice when the tremors turned from being a nervous condition to a symptom of alcohol sickness), full of self-doubt and loathing for humanity. Sober Vladimir was a frail slip of a man tangled inside a towering mass of tissue and bone. Drunken Vladimir, while still bitter, at least had the sense to speak up for himself. He had the ability to talk about something other than science or medicine. Sober Vladimir longed for things like a woman's hair slipping over his stomach or the touch of soft skin against his face. Drunken Vladimir, on occasion, could acquire such pleasantries, though sadly, he was usually too drunk to fully appreciate them.

The sound of tumbling pebbles shook him loose from his own head. "*Salut?*" Again, nothing responded but his own voice. He sat up and rubbed his face, pushing his fingers hard against his eyes. It was still dark when he opened them, except for the pressure-induced rings of bright white and red that rippled through the space in front of him. *I have no idea where I am,* he thought. *I was having dinner with that family and then I was here. Who are those people? Why did the man... Alexander? Alexandru? Why did he bring me here? What could they possibly want from me?* He laid back again on the rock. *Unless he wants me to do terrible things to that girl of his, then I don't know what I could possibly do for him.* This made him laugh. Drunken Vladimir had a sense of humour. He hoped that Sober Vladimir was paying attention.

The sound came again, louder this time. Chills ran through Vladimir, the kind that only happen when someone's really there. "Luca?" He could not conceal the urgency in his voice.

"Were you hoping it would be?"

If he lived to be a hundred, he would never forget that heavy velvet voice. It was too sultry for a young woman. Voices like that took years of cultivation.

"How did you find me?"

"I followed you. I was sitting on the path above you all of this time."

It was torture to hear her voice so close, but see nothing; just the way the sea had done to him. "You've just been watching me lay here?"

"No, it is too dark to see. I was listening to you call out my brother's name. Then I listened to you laughing. And when you were done doing that, I just listened to you breathe."

"Your family will be looking for you, I expect. You should go back." *Because if you stay, child, I may do something I will regret...*

"They won't be looking for me. They know I followed you. They *want* me to follow you. Except for Luca. He despises you already. And my grandmother—though she does not trust most people."

Vladimir chuckled. "What are you talking about?"

"*Oh...* you don't know, do you? My father didn't tell you why you are here, then?"

Veda moved in closer, close enough that Vladimir could see her now. In the darkness, her skin appeared to be shadowed with shades of deep indigo and blue. He wanted so badly to put his mouth on that skin and taste her.

"He brought you here so you would take me back to Moscow with you."

"Why do you have to go to Moscow?" he replied hazily.

She sighed. "No, Mister. It does not matter where you *take* me. He just wants you to take me with you. He wants to give me to you."

"But...I just met you. I don't even know you. He doesn't know *me*..." he put his hand to his forehead. "And why does your brother despise me?"

"He's going to give you money to take me. Of course, we'll have to marry. He won't pay you if you don't marry me."

"*What?*"

"And Luca...well, that's a long story. He is my twin. To say it simply, we are close because of that and he doesn't want me to leave him," she explained matter-of-factly.

29

"Perhaps, then, he should be angry with your father!" He felt sick again. "And your grandmother hates me, too? What have I done?"

"She has her reasons, but never mind that." Veda felt sorry for him then. He was just a poor drunken man thrust into this mess. "Listen to me, Vladimir Millerovo. I am only telling you what I know. You can leave tonight if you wish. You owe my family nothing. If you don't want me, then don't take me. Do you understand?"

"No, I *don't* understand! I mean..." his Romanian was slipping again, "...I understand, eh... arranged marriages, but this... this is as though your father went to the market to buy you a husband!"

"Listen, Mister... I told you, if you don't want me then go. No harm will come to you. In fact, it would make my brother and grandmother very happy to see you go."

He moaned and rubbed his face again. His hair stood straight up at the front of his head like a madman's. "I didn't mean to say that I don't want you..."

"It's probably better that you go, anyway." Veda turned her face away from him.

He grabbed her by the arms. "Now you listen to me. I didn't say I didn't want you..."

"You just don't want to marry me."

"No. I just don't know you. That is all. And you don't know me. Don't you think it might be good to know each other before you run away to Moscow with me?"

"So you *do* want me then?" She came in closer to him, leading his arms around her as she moved.

She smelled so good to him. She was soft and warm and standing with her breasts so very near to his face. He rested his hands on the small of her back while she ran her hands slowly up the length of his thighs. And now, of course, he was sobering up. Now he was really here in the dark, on a bed of rocks, with a beautiful woman caressing him, offering herself to him, and the sea creeping in around them.

"You're trembling," she whispered.

Of course he was trembling. That is what Sober Vladimir did.

"What's wrong Mister Millerovo? I love saying your name. *Mill-ehr-hovo*," she twirled it around with her tongue. "Don't they have women like me in Moscow?"

"Yes…but one usually has to pay for the pleasure of their company."

She recoiled as though he'd slapped her and then attempted to conceal her hurt with an indignant smile. "You would know a great deal about that, then?"

Vladimir lowered his head and ran his hand through a dishevelled mass of his brown hair. "I apologize. Truly, I don't want to do this, Veda. You are a beautiful and intelligent girl. You should go home." He hated himself more than ever in that moment. *My impotency drives me to cruelty, my sweet girl. Go home now before I ruin you, too.*

"I understand," she whispered and cast her eyes down to the ground. "I enjoyed listening to you breathing, Mister Millerovo." And then she turned away.

Before he could think better of it, he spoke. "Veda…it's not…" he inhaled deeply to keep his voice from shaking. "It's just that…I am not a good man." If it had been brighter, had there been a moon in the sky, she would have seen that he was close to tears.

"Well, I knew *that* the moment you came into our home," was all she said before walking away.

There was no sleep for Veda. She lay stiffly on her bed, circled by a hundred different thoughts like vultures, unable to sort them into any reasonable order. There was no telling which one would take her eyes or just pick over her bones. Things hadn't gone the way she'd planned. She was supposed to be the one to reject his proposition, she was supposed to feel resistant to the whole thing, knowing that eventually she would submit to her father's wishes. Then everything would be set right.

She remembered when she was very young, Iona told her a story about a beautiful young girl who was blessed by God with the gift of *vision*—not visions seen with her eyes, but with her mind. The girl was kept safe her whole life because she always paid attention to her visions. Then one day, the devil came to her, in the form of a stranger. The girl knew that he was really the devil, but she also knew that her visions had always led her down the necessary path. Even though her vision showed her a terrible end with the devil, it was the end that God had chosen for her. The girl knew the only way to keep things right was to walk God's path, even if she held the hand of the devil the whole way. She remembered asking her grandmother why God would want the girl to walk with the devil. Iona only said that it was not for them to question God's way, only to believe that there was a greater purpose. Veda had nightmares for many years about the girl and the devil. She was certain that if the devil ever came to her, she would run far away with Luca. She would be safe then. Luca would keep her safe. And if God would damn her for her disobedience, then so be it. His punishment could be no worse than the consequences of giving herself to evil.

But now, the devil was waiting on the rocks by the sea. He did not want her, even when she had touched him the way she had. He could have taken her right then and there, but instead he told her to go home. What manner of devil has a conscience? Surely such a thing was impossible; unless, of course, it was a trick. Maybe he was trying to trick Veda into thinking him a decent man, so she would want him even more. Veda lay on her bed, thinking and staring at the colourful woven curtains that divided the small house into private sleep-ing quarters. She gazed sleepily at the beautiful, billowing walls of cloth and thought that if it was a trick, then it was working.

꩜

Just before the dawn, when it was just light enough for him to see, Vladimir dragged his bones back up to the house. It was his intent to thank Alexandru and

Lavinia for their kindness and then go back to his room in town. He couldn't even be certain what happened last night. His scattered recollection of events had all the makings of some erotic nightmare, the kind that Vladimir had been plagued with since he was a boy. Perhaps that was all last night had been anyway. He could hold onto that hope for the next few minutes at least.

As he reached the top of the hill, several things came into view. The little house, *(Veda is in there, black hair unbound, her body soft and loose in a state of dreaming...dreaming of me? God, please let her be dreaming of me...)* a small group of sheep grazing on the hill, the reddish cliffs beyond, and Luca under a gnarled tree. Vladimir hesitated and then approached with caution. He nodded to the boy, but was met with nothing but the silence of deep, black eyes.

"You'll no doubt be pleased to know that I am leaving today," Vladimir said quietly, after finding the courage to open his dry mouth.

Again, Luca said nothing. His square jaw and drawn cheekbones tightened, casting more shadows over his already intense face. Veda wore the same shadows on her face.

"I meant no harm by coming here. You should know that." Vladimir began to walk away.

"You look too old to have just finished school, as you said," he replied, ignoring Vladimir's peace offering. His voice was just as sultry and thick as Veda's.

"It took me longer than most as I had some...personal situations that required me to take leave at one point."

"You look not so much younger than my mother."

"I am twenty-seven, since it seems to be a concern of yours."

"Did your 'personal situations' have anything to do with your drinking, Mister Millerovo?"

Here was a difference. When Veda said his name it sounded like a piano trill, like a beautiful sonatina. When Luca said it, he said it with such contempt that it sounded like a vulgar curse.

"I don't see where that is any business of yours."

"You were very drunk last night."

"Did you follow me, as well?"

"I was already out here. Anyway, you carry yourself like a man who drinks to hide something."

"That's very profound. Now, I'm going to find your father and say goodbye. It's been a pleasure, Luca."

"If only it were so simple, Mister Millerovo. You'll be back for her. She's your salvation," Luca said with calm resignation as Vladimir staggered on and away.

As Veda promised, Vladimir was able to walk away from the Sera family without any trouble. No harsh words were exchanged, no curses laid upon him by Iona *(how can you curse the devil?)*, no threat of physical harm by any of the brothers. Alexandru was filled with a mix of sadness and relief; he knew from the start there would be no simple end to it. The family was right back where they started, or they would have been had Veda been able to forget her brief liaison with the Russian.

But Veda would never forget the way she felt as she set off to finish, if nothing else, what had been started at the rocks. It had not been so difficult to find him; Constanta was not yet such a popular holiday destination, and the presence of a stranger did not go unnoticed. She carried out her investigation at dusk, while the marketplace emptied out and the vendors were closing up their carts for the night. The perimeter of the square, which was lined with houses and inns, was still alive with the music and laughter of families. If Vladimir were to stay anywhere, it would be here, where there were always rooms for rent. Veda wandered from house to house, inquiring about the Russian guest.

He was staying in a small, third floor apartment that faced the sea. She shook as she climbed the stairs. Veda knew what she'd come for and was certain that she could get it. When she and Luca had been together, of course it was pleasurable, but there was no mystery. They had bathed together, slept in the same bed. Their hands were not foreign to each other's body. Making love to Luca was an act of bonding, more than an act of passion. But this was different. She longed to know what Vladimir looked like without his clothes. She wanted to feel his strong hands, she wanted to touch him again, as she'd done so briefly on the beach. Veda was aroused before she reached his door, so how terribly disappointed she must have been to find no one there.

Patience was no companion of Veda's. Perhaps she would have been content to wait by the door had it been locked, but since that was not the case she did not hesitate to enter. The room was very small and plain. There was a table and chair in the corner, and an unmade bed. A gaslight burned by the window. Though it was night, Veda could tell that the view more than compensated for the simplicity of the quarters. There was a canvas bag on the table and Veda casually glanced through its contents. Garments, mostly, though wrapped within them were a few bottles of a clear liquid that Veda assumed to be spirits.

She sat down on the bed, and then laid back, nestling into the groove that Millerovo had left in the mattress. It was a good deal larger than she. She pressed her face into the place where his head had been and inhaled deeply. It smelled of sweat and liquor, the way Vladimir had at supper. She closed her eyes and retraced their moment on the beach, only this time he didn't send her away. This time he didn't let her go.

⸙

Imagine Vladimir's bewilderment and surprise upon returning to his room, drunk, and finding *her* fast asleep in his bed. Beautiful Veda curled up in the very spot where he'd pleasured himself after half of a bottle of drink, thinking of *her*. Oh, this was a grand thing, indeed.

"Why, it must be my birthday," he whispered sleepily.

Veda jumped, drawing herself upright, her heart ricocheting off the walls of her chest. "I…I was just…"

"Sleeping?" he smiled. "Was your bed unsuitable, so you came to try mine?"

Veda stood up. She was struck by the way he filled the entire length of the doorway. His clothes were rumpled and stained, the very same he'd worn the day before. There was a dusting of light brown hair across his chin and jaw. The hair on his head stuck out in every direction, stiff with a concoction familiar to all drunks—sweat, saliva, and liquor—and occasionally vomit, but not on this night, not yet.

"You left the door unlocked."

"Obviously. What are you doing here, Veda?"

"Waiting for you," she said with complete innocence.

"Well, here I am." He held out his arms, presenting himself. "Now you've seen me, you can go."

It took Veda every bit of restraint to keep from crying. "I don't understand you, Mister Millerovo. When I look into your soul, I can see that you want me as much as I want you. But all you say is that I should go home. What would it take? Next time should I be waiting naked in your bed? Would that have made a difference?"

"Why do you want me, Veda?" He removed his waistcoat and threw it to the floor. "Is it because I just happened to be the one that your father brought home? I could have been anyone. Are you so desperate to scratch that *itch*, Veda, that you'd lay down for any stranger that would cross your path?"

"You are a most offensive man, Mister Millerovo. I am not a whore."

"You certainly aren't chaste," he scoffed, "even that voice of yours is immodest."

Veda straightened up. She was very tall for a woman, all legs and neck. "No. I have been with a man. *One* man. If that makes me a whore, so be it. But I am an honest whore, unlike most women who would swear to their innocence no matter how many times they've had their *'itches'* scratched, as you say."

"Veda," he put his hand to his head and rubbed his eyes, "have you happened to notice that we don't really get along very well?"

"It's a fine, silken thread between love and hate, Mister Millerovo. And I get along with you fine. You just don't get along with me."

"Really, child…there are hundreds of young men in this city. If you are in such great need of a husband, I doubt very much it would be a problem for you to find one."

"I didn't come here to persuade you to marry me. I didn't come here because you 'just happened to be the one my father chose,' as you say. I was happy living my life with my family and then my father decides I need to go and just like that, I'm expected to marry a stranger and go far away from everything and everyone I love! So, because I *do* love my family I agreed without any trouble to do as my father wished and believe me, Mister Millerovo, I had no intention of actually caring for you. My brother, whom I love more than anything in this world, hates you, my grandmother thinks you are the devil, you say hurtful things and you drink too much, but here I am," Veda took a deep breath. "I am here because I cannot stop thinking of you."

Vladimir swallowed hard. He watched the skin around her nose and mouth turn from a soft olive to a heart-wrenching shade of pink.

"Veda, I think you may have mistaken me for a different sort of man. I apologise if I misled you, and for wasting your family's generosity and time."

Veda stared at the floor to keep from crying, at a loss for words. When she was able, she collected herself and went to the door, pushing past Vladimir.

"Goodnight, Mister Millerovo. I'll not be bothering you again."

And she was gone. Vladimir slumped against the door frame, listening to the echo of her feet hitting stone. His head was spinning and he wondered if any of the past few minutes had been real. It couldn't have been. He would have been a fool to let that brilliant creature go…no, he didn't just let her go, he *made* her go. He *made* her go. He nearly killed himself stumbling down the stairs and running carelessly into the dark market square. Her name swirled all around him as he desperately called after her.

When he caught her, she was on the dirt road, weeping. It wasn't as though she was in love with Millerovo, but she was hurt and ashamed. She was ashamed of the way she'd thrown herself at this man; ashamed of the rejection he'd returned. Now, how could she go home and face her father? How could she explain that she wasn't good enough for a drunken stranger? How could she tell her father that the man would rather turn away his dowry than marry her? She was ruined for anyone now, probably even Luca.

She thought about the path. Where was God trying to lead her now? There was no path she could see before her. Not now, not anymore. Maybe the only path now led to the sea. There were gods in the sea. If she could not follow God in Heaven's path, then maybe she could drown, giving herself to those gods instead. She thought she might go to Iona, perhaps she'd know what to do now that the devil had sent her back home for a second time.

But he caught her. More accurately, he almost knocked her to the ground. She steadied herself and reached for him as he fell to his knees and vomited.

"Veda," he gasped between heaves, "Veda, forgive me. I am a wicked man," he spat and collapsed on all fours.

Veda knelt beside him and brushed his hair from his wet face. She held him and tenderly rubbed his back as he purged the last of the vodka from his stomach.

"Oh, god…Veda, please take me home," he whispered to the dirt.

And that was what she did.

They did not make love that night. Instead, Veda took him back to his room and washed the filth from his face and body. She undressed him and helped him into bed, then put out the light. She did not undress fully, but removed her bodice and overskirt and lay down next to him. She barely slept through the night; her rapid heartbeat made it much too difficult.

At dawn, Veda opened her eyes after one of only a few intermittent periods of light sleep. Vladimir was still in a deep slumber behind her. He was holding on to her tightly, fearful of losing her even in a state of dreaming. She tried to shift slightly beneath his long, solid arm and he pulled her in even closer to his body. He moaned softly, though his rhythmic breathing did not change. He was still asleep when he moved his hand to Veda's breast and began to unconsciously grind himself against her back. As the movements of their bodies grew quicker and more voluntary, Veda feverishly removed the rest of their clothes, so when Vladimir was fully awake they were both naked and writhing against one another. He was mostly inside of her, still erect for several moments before sober panic crept upon him and he went flaccid. Veda tried to resurrect him, but the sunlight spilling through the window exposed Vladimir in a way that was far too real and shameful. He had no shadows to hide him, no alcohol to numb him. What he saw was a golden angel, naked and glistening, straddling his stinking body, kindly hiding her disappointment in the useless piece of meat between his legs.

"Veda, I'm sorry…I can't…" he was practically choking on his shame. "I can't…unless I drink. I don't know why…I'm sorry…"

But Veda smiled at him. It was a sincere and loving smile. "Mister Millerovo…do not be sorry." She bent down and kissed him on the mouth. "Tonight, we drink."

She had slipped home through the first wave of townspeople, unnoticed. Her father and older brothers would have gone to the boats already. Lavinia and Iona would be waiting for her, but she could handle them. They were women, they would understand, but Veda knew that even though her father wanted her to be with Vladimir, he would not approve of their carnal behaviour prior to marriage. More importantly, it would be enough provocation for her older brothers to hunt Millerovo down and teach him a morality lesson. All of this was easy enough to predict, but it would be her dealings with Luca that worried her the most. She had no idea how he would be or what she could possibly say to him. He'd shut her out since Millerovo's arrival, no doubt to punish her for betraying him. She feared things would never be the same between them.

Of course, it was Luca she first encountered upon her return that morning. He was chopping wood behind the house as she approached.

"Good morning." She ran her fingers through her unkempt hair.

"No, not really." He didn't look at her.

"It wasn't a question."

"My mistake," he said.

Veda watched him for a moment. His muscles were rigid and tense as he brought down the axe again and again. She felt a bizarre mix of sympathy and lust wash through her as he worked. His beautiful skin was shimmering. "Luca, are you ever going to look at me again? Are you ever going to understand this?"

"I don't know. Were you with him last night? Because if you were, then, no. I don't think I can look at you and I *certainly* can't understand."

"I wouldn't treat you this way if you fell in love with another woman, you know."

Luca violently struck the tree stump with his axe and let go. It was a shame to see the rage in his face on such a beautiful day. The sky was a surreal blue and a clean wind came in from the sea.

"You love him?" he choked.

"Oh, Luca... *no*. I didn't mean it that way. I only meant to say..."

"So you're just spreading your legs for him then? Is *that* what you meant to say?"

She didn't bother to answer. There was nothing she could say that wouldn't hurt him.

Tears fell from his face. "I suppose he was better at it than I. I'm certain you were not his first."

"Luca, don't do this. I will not compare you to him."

"No, Veda. I just need to know." He moved toward her and put his hands on her shoulders. "It's a simple question. Who pleased you more?"

Veda had never, not in all their years, been afraid of her twin, but now the look in his tearful, wild eyes and the way he gripped her flesh terrified her. She could see in the mirror that was her brother's face an ugliness she'd not thought possible, in Luca or in herself. Luca had always been her mirror. She had prayed since they were very young that he'd not die before her, as looking upon his lifeless body would be no different than seeing her own death. Now, there was something malevolent in his eyes and Veda knew that it could only mean that she, too, had the capacity for such rage and sadness. He was trying to read her thoughts and she was too frightened to stop it. She'd never needed to stop it before.

"Luca, please. This is not like you…"

His face relaxed and a smile spread slowly across it. "Or perhaps he wasn't as much of a man as you thought, eh?" He pulled her close, and kissed her on the jaw. "If you like, I can finish the job for him."

Veda leaned back, unable to comprehend what her brother had become in that moment. She felt the sparks shooting between them, but this time they were different. They were burning her skin, and when she cast her eyes down to the place where their bodies met, she saw that they had gone from blue to a painful red.

"*Luca!*" Iona's deep voice sliced through them and Luca stepped back from his sister. The old woman came forward a few paces, her eyes fixed on her grandson. She was moving slowly and purposefully, her shadow creeping upon the boy, towering over him, threatening to swallow him until he was small and afraid. "Are you finished with the wood yet? I have other chores for you, child. If you do not choose to fish alongside your father and brothers then you must work for me here, *da*?" Her voice was calm and soft.

Veda was motionless by a tree; long, black strands of hair pasted to the wet trails left by her tears. Luca was breathing heavily. There was no wind now. The space around them was utterly still.

"Forgive me, grandmother. I'm almost done here," he said.

Iona smiled and nodded at him. She turned to Veda and held out her hand. "Come on, girl. Come inside with me." Veda grasped her grandmother's hand as though she were a young child again. She did not look back as her brother swung the axe, splitting the log in two. She did not have to look at him to know that he was imagining the wood to be Vladimir.

But Luca could not hate her, and he could not begrudge her his love for much longer. She was *Veda*, beautiful and shimmering. She was of his olive flesh and he of hers. And although things were never the same for the twins after that, the day Veda and Vladimir left for Moscow, Luca pulled her aside and quietly gave her a reluctant blessing. She swore that she would always keep him in her heart and she knew that she would never forget that brilliant blue light that once held them so close, but neither could pretend that a dreadful rift wouldn't exist between them for the rest of their lives. And Luca could not hide the fear he felt for his sister as the devil took her far away to a cold, foreign life.

On the train to Moscow, the situation settled heavily in Veda's belly. She watched from the window as field turned to hill and hill turned to mountain. What a remarkable thing it was to be travelling so quickly inside such a massive contraption. She'd never seen anything like it before. When it was dark, she watched her fiancé as he dozed next to her. She watched his chest rise and fall; she watched his fingers and the spindly bones in his hands twitch and his eyes flutter beneath brown and purple-hued lids. They had successfully made love twice before leaving Constanta; unsuccessfully, three times. There was some hope for Veda to cling to; on one of the two successful occasions Vladimir had only consumed half of a bottle, not enough to leave him completely intoxicated. There were some precarious moments, but Veda was not left disappointed. But as she looked on him now she realized that she knew nothing about the man beside her. Perhaps *nothing* was a bit erroneous; she knew he was a chemist. She knew he was a drunk. She knew he suffered from myriad dysfunctions and evils and soon she would be living with him and his ills as one big happy family in a dense, frigid city far from her loved ones, far from the sea, far from warmth. Her family wouldn't even be present for their wedding. She would marry Vladimir in a strange church, in a strange city, surrounded by…more strangers, or his family and friends? Did he even have any family or friends? Did he have the means to support her? And what of children? What would they do when the money her father had given them was gone? She placed her head against the window, seeing nothing but her reflection as the darkness sped by and tried to remember to breathe. Her grandmother said that it would be God's will that she walk with the devil, so she'd walked with, slept with, and now travelled on a train with the devil. The world was, indeed, made of mysteries. She fondled the little wooden cross that hung around her neck and prayed that Iona was right.

Many months later, Veda would lose the necklace on a dark Moscow street, under an embankment of snow. She was devastated, but held her tears from her husband for fear that he would, in an inebriated state and with the kindest intentions, purchase a replacement; one that they could not afford. The necklace was handmade by her grandfather, Iona's late husband, and there were only two in existence. The other belonged to Luca.

Moscow, 1868

The vagrant was awake when Vladimir returned home that night, but still he sprawled his rag-covered bones directly in the path to the stairs. Vladimir never really minded stepping over him when he was unconscious, but times like these were different. He saw it as some sort of violation, though he couldn't decide whom it violated more.

"Pardon me," Vladimir muttered.

"Don't think I could if I wanted to," the man replied with a voice like gravel, then chuckled.

Vladimir climbed over him, staying close to the end with the feet. "Did you come with this building as part of the architectural design or are you just one of those little superfluous pleasantries, like the rats, that make this place worth its rent?"

"If I was you, I'd not be so quick to pass judgement on me. It's only a small matter of stairs between your life and mine, eh?" He smiled, displaying his few rotting teeth still attached to gum.

Vladimir peered over his shoulder at his pitiful adversary. "And if I were you, I'd not be so quick to insult the same man that you implore to give you coins and bread, beggar."

The vagrant grunted and sputtered, referring to Vladimir as swine, only after he heard Millerovo's door open, then close again.

Once inside, the warmth that Vladimir's beautiful wife radiated melted his troubles. If only he could stay in this room always, never to feel the cold streets outside again. He wanted to stay here with her until winter's end, and then take her away. He wanted to see her glowing in the sun, the way she had in Constanta. He wanted to see her swimming in warm waters. He had no business stealing her from her home.

~⋛~

Your mother was amazing to me then. As stubborn as she was at times, she never complained about our life. She spent her days weaving the most beautiful tapestries for our walls, and blankets to keep us warm. It was miraculous, the way she turned our dreary room from a prison cell to a luxurious parlour. She always used hues of red ~ she was convinced that the colour red would keep us safe. If I were ever to believe in magic, it would have been because of Veda. I had no doubt that she would be an incredible mother to you.

"I received a letter from my mother today," Veda happily informed her husband before he even removed his coat and hat. "That makes two since I sent word of our baby."

"Well, then it's been a thrilling day for us both. You received a letter and I, after a mind-numbingly futile day at work, had a quarrel with that filth monger that pollutes our stairwell," Vladimir replied.

Veda, undeterred, wrapped her arms around him. "And now, here you are, home with your beautiful wife. All men should be so lucky," she laughed.

"Ah, you're right. Don't pay me any mind." He returned her affectionate embrace, kneading the flesh on her back with his hands and burying his face in her hair. "I'm in a wretched mood."

"It's because of the letter, isn't it?"

"Why would you think that?"

"Does it not sadden you that my mother has written us twice while yours has not responded at all?"

"It comes as no great surprise."

"She'd still speak to you if it weren't for me, and for that I am sorry. I didn't want her to hate me."

"She doesn't hate you, Veda. She has yet to even meet you face to face. She just..."

"She just wishes you hadn't married into my family."

"Veda, that's not it..."

"She called us gypsies!"

"She hoped I would marry…closer to the family. That's their way." The thought made Vladimir as uncomfortable now as it had when he was young.

"My family works very hard for what they have. We're not thieves!"

"I know."

"The implication sickens me, you know."

"Yes, I know."

"Gypsies!" Veda spat, shaking her head. "I can think of no greater insult to my family's honour."

Vladimir simply nodded, knowing that the only thing to do was to allow her to carry on until she burned out. There was nothing more to be done once the tirade turned from Russian to Romanian.

"Of course she won't write to us now. I imagine it must burn her terribly to think of her future half-gypsy grandchild! Ha! I hope we make one hundred babies, so all over this country people will know of them and say, 'Oh, did you hear about all of those gypsy babies that were born?' and they'll say, 'Oh, yes—I hear they are the grandchildren of Nalia and Viktor Millerovo! Can you imagine?' What a scandal it would be then, eh?"

"It would be scandalous, indeed." Vladimir muttered absently. "We'd have to move to a larger apartment."

"What are you talking about?" Veda suddenly became aware of her husband's voice.

"If we had a hundred babies." He was too tired to be serious now. "Where ever would we keep them all?"

"I'm glad this is funny for you," Veda sneered. "What do you know about disgrace, anyway?"

Although he knew Veda hadn't truly meant what she said, rather she had no real understanding of the matter, Vladimir grinned because it was the only thing he could do that would mask his contempt.

"Nothing, my love. I know nothing about disgrace."

But Vladimir knew disgrace most intimately. Disgrace had been his only child-hood friend. Disgrace had given him his first wet kiss and his first anxious touch below the waist, but Veda had no way of knowing this. In truth, Vladimir had fabricated most of what Veda knew about his family and childhood in order to appease his inquisitive bride. He could not claim a completely normal upbring-ing; his drinking and intimacy troubles shattered that illusion from the start, yet he could not provide Veda with any reasonable explanation for his ills. Fortunately, Veda hadn't pressed the affair. After all, she'd left a demon of her own back in Constanta.

As far as Veda knew, Vladimir's aristocratic parents severed all financial and personal ties with their son when they learned of his marriage to a 'gypsy woman,' as Nalia Millerovo had allegedly called her. This was the story Vladi-mir told his new wife when he returned from a visit to his family's home. That was nearly two years ago now, and Vladimir hadn't spoken to his mother or his father since.

What Veda didn't know was that Vladimir never arrived at his family's house that night. Instead, he spent the evening drinking in a pub and ended the night at a disreputable inn with a dishonourable woman where upon arrival to his room he promptly passed out and spent the night alone on the cold floor. By morning, the woman and what little money he had was gone, as was the pocket watch given to him by his father. He could live without these things; at the very least he still had his fidelity and could return to his wife with a semi-clear conscience, despite his original intentions. There was a cavernous space within him reserved for such discarded duplicitous thoughts.

In fact, Vladimir had not spoken to his parents since the spring of 1861, which was not coincidentally the semester in which he found himself taking sabbatical from university. It was the spring of Vladimir's first fully developed mental collapse. He was twenty-two years old then, and halfway through his fourth year. It was such a shame that Vladimir should fall *ill* at that juncture; he had just begun to really learn what research was about. This was the year that books would be replaced with real, tangible medicines, the year that theory would become practice. But when Vladimir took leave, against the advice of all but one of his professors, he caused irreparable damage to his future career. The momentum he built in those first years would later be impossible for him to regain, a fact that resulted in numerous disciplinary actions, several harrowing university board reviews, and the ultimate retardation of his scholarly advancement.

By the time Vladimir was ready to begin his own research, most of his colleagues had already begun to make names for themselves within the community, and there was little friendship to be found in the viciously competitive field.

In a sense, Vladimir Millerovo had unwittingly made a name for himself as well, though it would be most unfortunately associated with excessive drinking and mental incompetence. So, really, it mattered very little whether or not positions as research assistants were plentiful or scarce; Vladimir was considered a liability, and for all of this, he reasoned, he had his parents to thank.

There was very little about Vladimir that could not be excused by his upbringing. In 1837, his father Viktor Millerovo II was a wealthy thirty-one-year-old bacchanalian who essentially abducted his then thirteen-year-old cousin Nalia Khiva for the purpose of renting her to other wealthy drunks, under the guise of aristocratic tradition. No one in the family objected to Nalia acting as a cultural envoy, an escort to the theatre and ballet, a courtesan. In fact, Viktor took great care of his young cousin, despite his vices. He kept her healthy and beautiful, and provided her with an impeccable education. She excelled in the arts and grew into a charming woman, as well as a fine and loving mother, all by the age of fifteen.

Viktor officially wed Nalia in 1839, less than four months before she gave birth to their son, despite the fact that there was a good chance that the child was not his. Viktor's rationale was that even if the child did not belong to him,

Nalia *did,* and that would be good enough for him. The baby would be known as a Millerovo whether it was biologically true or not, although Viktor's uncertainty about the bloodline was strong enough to deny the child the honour of being called Viktor III.

Many years later, as young Vladimir entered adulthood, the issue would be settled. He was the mirror image of Viktor, but by then it was far too late to change the young man's name.

London, 1887

Red was the colour of Veda's favourite thread and her mouth, and black were her eyes and hair. Olive was for her skin, and amber was for the sky at dusk in Constanta. Amber was also the colour of whiskey and rum. Blue was for Veda's beloved Black Sea and for the Caribbean, as seen from the mountainous rain forest, which brings to mind green, which was also for the estate in Martinique where young Ana would play and presently, for the fairy in the absinthe that Vladimir was about to consume. Soon, one of Pinkney's girls would arrive and he would consume her, too.

He'd written all he could for the day, and now that night was upon the city there would be little to comfort the insomniac other than strange flesh and chemicals. He despised having to rely on Pinkney for aid, but it was the only option. After a particularly feral evening a few months earlier, the heavily drugged Russian confessed to Pinkney many incriminating events from his past. Since then, the lecherous rat kept Vladimir in his pocket, insisting that he deal only with him regarding all matters of corruption and decadence.

He was thinking…thinking about what? The bottle in his hand was half drained, he really couldn't think too clearly about anything after that. Then there was a knock, which was something concrete for him to ponder for a moment.

He must have said 'come in' or something of that nature, because the door opened and there were light footsteps approaching his bed. He opened his eyes to see.

"'Ello…Mister Millerovo?" a soft voice cooed with a bit of hesitation.

"Have I died?" Vladimir slurred. He was looking at Veda. She was young again—not that she ever got so old—and her shimmering black hair spilled forward over her shoulders. Her skin was whiter than he recalled, but such was the nature of ghosts and angels, as he'd heard it told. He thought he smelled the Black Sea drifting in through his window. It was salty and sweet, not at all like the usual rank odour of the Thames. He'd died and gone back to Constanta to be with his bride. Maybe there was a God after all.

"No, you're not dead. You've had quite a time of it with this bottle, it seems, but you're definitely not dead." The girl smiled and placed her hand between his legs, massaging him until he was hard. "See? Very much alive," she purred.

"You're not Veda, are you?" He swallowed hard to keep from vomiting.

"I can be whoever you like."

"There is no one I like." He was close to tears, and then he could see her better. She looked so young, cleaner than the usual girls. "How old are you, child?"

If this was that little girl, the one Pinkney tried to pawn off on him earlier, there was going to be a world of pain in store for the reprobate…once Vladimir was sober enough to stand again.

She claimed to be seventeen, and since there was no way or reason to dispute it, he proceeded to take her so brutally that she nearly lost consciousness.

❧

I know, dear Ana, that this subject is most inappropriate for a father to discuss with his daughter, but I feel it is the only proper way I can help you to understand me. You are my daughter, yes ~ but you are also my confessor, my salvation, my glorious redemption! Please do not feel compelled to act upon this ~ your very existence in this world is enough. So read these words, but do not fear for your purity and chastity. It is I who have sinned, and I am no better than those who once sinned against me. I thank whatever god there may be that you have had the strength to be a better soul than the rest of us. If there is a greater salvation than that found in our own minds, I am certain that it will be yours.

❧

When Vladimir was a very young boy, the presence of the courtesans in his lavish Moscow home presented no threat. The women were nothing but kind to him, fawning and doting over the precocious child as though he were a china doll. It would have never occurred to him at the time that these women, including his own mother, were mere children themselves, still fascinated by the prospect of having little breathing dolls of their very own to dress and love. Viktor and Nalia were bringing in girls so young, many of which had not yet become women in the physiological sense, 'because,' Viktor had declared, 'it was far easier to shape a vacuous child than a obstinate woman.'

Upon Vladimir's twelfth birthday, the obvious troubles of growing up in a whorehouse began to manifest and it was more than the adolescent could reasonably bear. There were beautiful women all around him, each and every day, remarking at what a handsome fellow he'd become. They were impressed and amazed at how tall he was for his age, and often commented on the emerging hairs that sprouted half-heartedly from his face. Nothing went unnoticed by the stable: not the beginnings of a muscle or a blemish on his skin, nor were the girls unaware of how he watched them. It was a petty little game they played with him—flaunting their corseted bodies, their uplifted breasts, speaking openly about their intimate experiences while they lifted their skirts to adjust a stocking or a garter, all the while pretending they didn't notice Vladimir's presence until—'*Oh my! We didn't see you there, Dimi! You weren't watching us, were you, pet?*' And they would bat their painted eyelashes and giggle madly while poor little '*Dimi*' (he detested that name) would stammer and blush and try to conceal his excitement until he could get away from them, escaping to his bedroom to relieve some of the tension in a most furious and sometimes painful manner, while the image of their bodies and the smell of their perfumes—his mother's included—were still fresh in his mind.

So over the years, young Vladimir would be exposed to many inappropriate things, though none so traumatizing as the girls' vicious teasing and the 'parties' that his parents frequently held. These soirees were nothing more than glorified auctions for the courtesans, fancy aristocratic getting-to-know-you sessions that would inevitably degenerate into drunken orgies. Vladimir would casually roam from room to room, silently observing the carnality that ensued and testing the contents of unguarded bottles and pipes. It would be only a matter of time before the vodka stopped burning his insides and the sweet smoke of opium no longer choked him, and he would develop a crippling taste for toxicity.

For all of the damage this newfound hunger would cause, it also sparked in the boy an interest in science, specifically chemistry. Vladimir had been schooled at home by his mother since he was five years old and had very little contact with other children as a result, which left him feeling very nervous about entering a real school for the first time. His mother, however, did not feel competent enough in the teachings of science and medicine to prepare him for university, if he was indeed that serious about it, so a private school would be the only option. In 1852, Vladimir was enrolled, ironically, into a very strict, very religious, college preparatory school. Of course, the headmasters were aware of the Millerovo family's reputation, but were generously able to over look the *rumours*, as the truth came to be known, after Viktor paid nearly twice the full cost of tuition.

It didn't take long for tales of the new student's home life to circulate, and the majority of Vladimir's classmates came to see him as some kind of hero, making the collective assumption that he was quite experienced with women, having had his pick of any number of them on a given evening. Vladimir didn't affirm these stories, though he did not deny them either. He simply maintained his normal quiet and humble composure and let the boys believe what they liked.

That spring, Viktor and Nalia took a holiday in Bombay, leaving Vladimir home with six of the courtesans for several weeks. Life was business as usual in the house: rich men came and went at all hours; the girls attended the theatre and ballet nightly, with numerous suitors; vodka and opiates were acquired and freely consumed by all. Yet, amidst it, the girls managed a tidy and orderly household, each taking turns at daily chores (Viktor didn't believe in employing servants) and minding Vladimir. They made sure that the boy completed his nightly studies, they fed him and washed his clothes and kept him company. They were all such good mothers to him then, it became very difficult for him to fantasize about them the way he always had.

It was a very confusing time for Vladimir as the novelty of motherhood quickly wore off for all concerned. Suddenly, the girls were less matronly and had resumed their teasing, which in turn thrust Vladimir back into the throes of frustration and desire. His thoughts became increasingly violent, though he seemed to be more withdrawn than ever. He dreamed of rape and murder so vividly that he would wake up screaming. He often dreamed of his mother; sometimes her body would be against his own, sometimes she would bathe him in a warm, clear pool, and she would touch him, and sometimes he merely dreamed of her luscious red mouth on him. As much as he loved these dreams, he despised them, as the girls were relentless in their torture upon washing his bedclothes. If only the girls could have known what dreadful thoughts were growing in the boy's poisoned mind.

Sonja was the first to break him, since Vladimir was too nervous and un-certain to do her any harm. The plump sixteen-year-old happened to be passing his room late one night just as he awoke in tears from a terrible dream. She held him and gently rocked him, kissing the top of his head, nuzzling her face in his soft brown hair as he held on to her tightly, his own face pressed into her large, pillow-like bosom. She wore only a white night dress, and he could feel her malleable flesh beneath the soft, thin fabric. Her dark copper hair was half bound, with long curly tendrils spilling over her shoulders. He was certain she'd just been with a man; he could still smell the sex on her. He knew that scent so well; it lingered throughout the entire house, just beneath the smell of a dozen perfumes.

"What's wrong, Dimi?" she had whispered to him in the darkness.

He said he'd had a frightening dream, to which she responded by pulling the blanket over them and twisting herself until their bodies were touching. She said she could make him forget about the dream, and then kissed him deeply on the mouth as she slid her thick hand under his nightclothes. After several moments in shock, Vladimir proceeded to imitate the rhythmic movements he'd once seen a stranger doing while on top of his mother, and he imagined he was doing quite all right when Sonja began to make the same breathy noises that he'd heard coming from Nalia.

Katya was the next in line once Sonja had shared the details of her conquest—and it was indeed considered a conquest. The girls had made a crude wager to see who would be the first to 'break in' Vladimir, one that had been running since the boy was eleven years old. Nalia was unaware of this at first, though upon finding out, her only words were, 'Oh, you cunning little tramps! Whoever it may be, teach him well. A man is nothing without a woman by his side, and there is only one certain way to keep her there.' The fiercely competitive Katya was convinced that she was better suited to 'teach' Vladimir. Sonja may have gotten to him first, but she was no teacher. She compensated for her sloppy technique by distracting her lover with her big, fleshy body parts; she possessed little grace and charm, and she was nowhere near as learned as the other girls. Sonja was nothing more than an easy, jiggling good time and it burned Katya to no end that this wanton court jester had beat her to the prize.

Seducing young Vladimir would be easy, especially for the beautiful Katya. Considered the gem of the house, she was one of Viktor's favourites, but Katya desired a challenge. She wanted Vladimir to come to her, but of all the courtesans,

Katya was the one who intimidated the thirteen-year-old the most. Day after day, Katya focused her kind attentions on Vladimir, going beyond the usual teasing to which he'd become accustomed and resorting to cruel, subtle manipulations. She would convince the boy that she was falling in love with him.

Her plan was a success, of course. Vladimir was young and Katya, while only two years older, was a very cunning and observant girl. She understood the boy, calling him by his proper name, instead of Dimi. "I know how you despise that name," she'd said sympathetically. "It's a child's name, and you are no longer a child."

She and Vladimir would find private corners of the house, away from the other girls, where they'd spend hours talking about all manner of things: books, music, dreams, religion.

Once, during a social gathering held after Viktor and Nalia had returned from India, Katya slipped away from the party to find Vladimir and keep him company. He was hiding in his room with a bottle of vodka, not yet fully intoxicated, though a bit more talkative than usual.

Katya took a seat next to him on the floor and put the vodka bottle to her lush pink lips. They sat in silence for a few moments, staring at the intricate designs on the carpet.

"You detest these parties, don't you?" Katya finally asked with her soft voice.

The boy nodded slowly and vacantly.

"Well, you aren't the only one."

Vladimir turned his eyes toward the girl, taken aback by her confession.

"Yes, you heard correctly. I loathe these events; all of us girls putting on our best pretences, flaunting ourselves the way we do and parading around like prized ponies. Truly I cannot stand having to pretend that I actually enjoy the company of those filthy old men."

"Then why do you do it?"

Katya smiled. "Because it's easy."

"Easy? But you're so smart. You read and write and sing. You're just as learned as the men…"

"And so what? If I were a man, all of that knowledge might do me some good, but as it is, no one really wants to listen to me speak of philosophy or politics unless I'm doing it without my clothes on. But at least this way I get to speak it. If I were to marry some arrogant young man, he'd certainly not allow me any ideas of my own."

"I wouldn't deny you your ideas."

"What are you talking about?"

"If you were to marry me—I mean, of course, when we were a bit older—I wouldn't make you keep quiet. You could study and learn anything you wanted. I'd let you do whatever you wished."

"Are you mad?" Katya laughed.

"Perhaps," Vladimir laughed in return.

"Oh, Vladimir. That's your problem: you are too kind." She reached for him and lightly brushed his cheek with her silken fingers. "If you're not careful, women will take advantage of you in the worst way."

"I'm careful," he replied with some uncertainty.

"Are you? I mean, consider what Sonja did to you."

Vladimir felt his face go hot.

"Certainly you've overheard enough of our conversations to know that we tell each other nearly everything."

"I know," the boy sighed and cast his eyes down to the floor again. "I suppose I just thought that it might be different since it was me."

Katya gazed at him sympathetically. "Oh, you poor, dear thing. Now do you see what I mean? It's dangerous for you to be so naïve. You're much like a precious little kitten amidst a pack of hungry wolves in this house." She leaned in closer to him, allowing the boy to take in the smell of her perfume and hoping that he would feel the heat that radiated from her skin. "Be wary of those girls. They just want to have their turns at breaking you in. They don't care about you...not the way I do."

"And how is it...that you...you care for me?" the boy stammered.

"I love you, Vladimir. I love you because I understand you and I want to protect you. I know it's not my place to profess thoughts such as these, but I think it would be a greater evil to keep the truth from you."

For Katya to say such things was the answer to Vladimir's prayers. At once, he felt the weight of his anger and frustration dissolve. The oppressive fantasies of violence that haunted him could cease now that his heart was so filled with goodness and love…and all because of this beautiful young creature before him. He thought he might burst as Katya kissed him deeply on the mouth and let him clumsily take her there on the floor of his bedroom.

Over the course of several weeks, Vladimir became obsessed with pleasing his new love. He did everything for her without question or complaint. He brushed her hair and fetched her food and drink and anything else she desired. He read to her and drew pictures for her when she was bored. He wrote poems and stories for her. Viktor and Nalia did not question their son's behaviour; it seemed only normal that a young man surrounded by young women would naturally develop the occasional infatuation. Katya managed to excuse herself from her normal activities by feigning a mysterious 'womanly' illness. Vladimir knew it was a ruse, one he thought she devised in order to preserve her loyalty to him.

But what Vladimir did not witness each night after he'd retire to his room was the passing around of his poems and love letters amongst the girls. They would giggle like little monsters as they mocked the boy's words.

"I told you I could have him eating out of the palm of my hand before any of you," Katya laughed and proclaimed proudly.

Sonja was not so impressed. "Please, Katya. Any one of us could have accomplished that if we tried. He's just a child. I do not see how it was any challenge."

"If it was so easy then why is it that he is at my beck and call and not yours? You had him first but I can't recall ever seeing him writing poems for you."

"So what?" Sonja scoffed. "So you have poems. What do you intend to do with him now that you have him wrapped around your finger?"

"Well, I've managed a pleasant little reprieve from my duties as a result. He's been the perfect accessory. The way he's been waiting on me hand and foot has been immensely helpful in convincing Viktor that I've been ill."

"So when do you plan to recover and go back to work?" a young girl called Greta asked.

"Soon, I suppose. I'm beginning to get restless. Innocent and awkward has been ever so much fun, but I miss strong and experienced. Young Vladimir does the best he can, but he is just a boy, after all."

At first, Vladimir was none the wiser to Katya's change of heart, which afforded him a few extra days of happiness before he discovered his one true love in the throes of passion with a forty-year-old banker. It would be an understatement to say that the young boy was devastated by this infidelity and, although he wouldn't know it at the time, this would be the origin of his lifelong subconscious hatred of the fairer sex.

London, 1887

"What are you writin'?"

Vladimir ignored the girl's sleepy voice. He didn't recall her having such an ugly accent the night before. Of course, the night before, she didn't speak to him with a British accent at all. He was certain she'd spoken like a Rom; she'd spoken like Veda.

The girl—he believed she called herself Mary—wrapped the blanket around her naked body and shuffled towards the desk where he was writing.

"Can I see?"

She leaned over his shoulder and in one quick move he closed the journal and pushed her away. Still, he did not speak.

She caught herself, nearly falling into the wardrobe behind her.

"That's fine, then. Can't hardly read, anyway," she scoffed to herself.

"It's none of your concern what I'm writing. It's not for you."

She made her way back to his bed, discarding the blanket and exposing herself. Again, Vladimir barely acknowledged her.

"Didn't expect you were writin' somethin' for me." She fell back onto the mattress and combed her fingers through a tangled mass of long, black hair. "It's for a girl, though, right?"

"Why would you think that?" Vladimir asked.

"'Cause I was watchin' you write and you had a look in your eyes... I seen that look in men's eyes before. Not that they'd be thinkin' of me, but they'd be thinkin' of someone they loved."

Vladimir raised his head to look at her. Save for the hair, she really didn't look like Veda at all. She looked worn and empty. Veda was never empty.

"No one's ever looked at you that way?" His voice was flat.

"Can't say they have," Mary replied.

She shrugged and looked down at her sprawled body, casually investigating the collection of small bruises on her legs and pelvis. Some were still fresh, courtesy of Vladimir, though he did not remember inflicting them upon her.

"Not even your father?"

Mary laughed. "Oh, there was somethin' for certain in me da's eye when he looked at me, but I wouldn't never 'ave called it love."

She drew the blanket over her thin torso and Vladimir thought he saw her blushing.

"I'm sorry...if your father hurt..."

"...Hurt me?" She looked him deeply in the eyes for a moment, silently telling him a long and terrible story, and then she glanced away. "Well, don't matter none anymore. He died last winter."

"Did he ever tell you..." Vladimir forced himself to swallow the painful lump in his throat. "I mean to say, did he ever say that he was sorry?"

"The only thing me da was ever sorry for was me bein' born."

A long, difficult silence filled the room. Mary wrapped herself tighter in the blanket and fidgeted with her hair, while Vladimir stared vacantly at the dirty floor beneath his desk, one hand fondling the absinthe bottle, the other resting limply on his thigh.

"It's for my daughter," he finally managed.

"What's that?"

"The book. It's a letter, actually, I'm writing for my daughter. A very long and difficult letter."

Mary straightened up, intrigued now. "You don't look like you'd be someone's father."

Vladimir grinned sadly. "I haven't been a very good one."

"If you were me da and you wrote a whole book for me, I'd think you was the best one to ever live."

"But you don't even know what it is I've written. It could be cruel and hateful lies."

"Don't matter, really. You're fillin' a book with words just for her and that's really quite special."

Vladimir hoped she was right. He looked at her again, softening his gaze, and simply said, "I'm sorry, Mary. I'm sorry if I hurt you."

She shrugged and stared vacantly toward the window. "It's just bruises. It's the marks you don't see that hurt most."

To this very day, Ana, I am shamed by my upbringing. It has been so long since I was that pathetic little boy, but I still see through his eyes. But I will not waste ink attempting to convince you or myself that I am not solely responsible for my behaviours and decisions since reaching manhood. And for that, I have shamed myself even more.

Surely you must know that your very existence has proven to me that I am not beyond hope. You see, I have despised women, deep within my mind and my heart for so long and with such fury that I became numb to it. I have felt no remorse for their pain or suffering. I have cared nothing for their thoughts or wishes. I have been empty within my heart and poisoned in my head and the only thing I have really ever concerned myself with are my own ugly desires. When I met your mother, I was empty still, but she sparked feeling in me for a while. This was her magic~ making me feel again. Of course, it did not last; she could only do so much and I had too many years of hatred behind me ... until you.

Still, I failed you. When you were born, it made me believe that there was goodness in the world, but there were so many difficult things surrounding Veda and myself at that time that I could not open myself to you the way I should have. You certainly would not recall how life was for us then, you were just an infant. I have never explained to you why we fled Moscow and travelled so far away from that life. You were too young to understand when we lived in Martinique, and you hated me so much by the time we left Étienne's home (do you remember Monsieur Étienne?) that I decided not to clutter your life any further with ir-relevant details of a time you don't even recall. In any case, it would not have altered your feelings for me and for my unforgivable actions, but here it is now ~ the series of events that led us down this profoundly tragic path.

After the incident with Katya, Vladimir was not himself. His studies began to suffer, and he did not eat or sleep regularly. His moods were severe and he no longer gazed adoringly upon the courtesans. He still watched them carefully, of course, but now it was through very different eyes. His behaviour became erratic, as well. There were numerous occasions in which he'd silently intrude upon the girls and their callers, standing still and quiet while the couple would be going at one another like wild beasts. It would be several minutes, usually, before he was noticed, at which time he would proceed to shriek obscenities at the pair. Viktor would punish the boy each time, but his outbursts did not cease until locks were installed on the bedroom doors. The girls were required to wear the keys on ribbons around their necks.

For the first time in his life, Vladimir was carefully monitored by his mother. The normally light-hearted Nalia became very concerned and serious when it came to matters involving her son. In fact, it was Nalia who first discovered *The Collection*, as it came to be called by the girls. *The Collection*, which was just that—a collection of the girls' personal belongings, along with several horrific drawings—was hidden in a wooden box beneath Vladimir's wardrobe. Inside there were a handful of torn pieces of women's undergarments, wads of hair extracted from brushes, handkerchiefs, single earrings and broken bits of glass. There were dried flower petals and a small stack of letters from Katya, though most of the words had been blackened out with ink. Lining the bottom of the box was a series of drawings depicting naked young women in all manner of torturous and pornographic situations, including strangulation by long ribbons with keys tied to the ends.

Nalia pleaded with her child to tell her why it had come to this, but his only response was to calmly say, "Because you are all whores. Vicious wolves and whores."

After a brief correspondence between Viktor and the headmaster of Vladimir's school, the child was sent away at once to live out the next five years in the dormitories.

⋙

In the spring of 1857, Vladimir marginally completed his final year at the preparatory, and returned home for a few months before beginning his first year at university. It was his first visit to the home in five years.

Time and a bit of distance had mended some of the rifts between he and his mother. Nalia had been a shallow woman for most of her son's life, but she was no longer blind to the fact that most of Vladimir's troubles could be attributed to his upbringing. Viktor, on the other hand, took the same apathetic position in relating to his troubled son that he always had, so really, there was little adjustment to be made by either party.

In those years, however, there were several changes within Viktor's stable. Some of the girls had left the house to marry and begin families, and some of the girls had simply left, not to be heard from again. New girls were brought in and trained, and by the time Vladimir returned home, only two girls from his childhood remained: Sonja, and a quiet, younger courtesan that Vladimir had few dealings with called Marta.

Nalia spoke to the young women regarding her son's return. It was explained to them how Vladimir was *a bit troubled* and had been sent away, and it was requested that they limit their contact with him to formal and public settings only. Once Nalia was out of range, Sonja provided the others with information that his mother had discreetly omitted. Of course, there had always been talk of Vladimir amongst the newer girls, but never had there been a reason to so thoroughly discuss him until his imminent homecoming.

The day of his return was marked with tension and anticipation. The girls waited on edge as Nalia paced through the parlor, fidgeting with her necklace and rings and hair. When he finally arrived, he was met by the pale faces of china dolls, wide-eyed and silent. Nalia did not hesitate to embrace her child, now a grown man, more than a full head taller than herself. Vladimir returned the gesture half-heartedly, not so much embracing his mother as lightly patting her on the back and hastily kissing her bright red lips.

Nalia held her son at arm's length and looked him over with great care. He did not do the same, only glancing at her enough to see that she didn't look a bit different than he remembered. She was still young and sharp and beautiful, just as she'd been in his dreams and nightmares.

Nalia was not as contented with what she saw before her. He'd grown tall and lean and that was well enough, but he looked so old. His cheeks were sunken and his bloodshot eyes were shrouded by heavy purple rings. His hair was a bit mussed, as were his clothes, but the thing that disturbed Nalia the most were his hands. They were large, and would have been strong if not for the incessant trembling. His fingers twitched uncontrollably at random intervals, his nails were bitten to the quick and the veins that ran to and from his arm were unnaturally raised and pulsating. His skin was rough and calloused and there were barely healed wounds on his knuckles and wrists.

"Dimi, what happened to your hands?"

"I'm studying to be a chemist, Mother. I use my hands a great deal," Vladimir replied coolly.

"Oh. I see." Nalia glanced away awkwardly, hurt by her son's tone. "Well, then. Let's get you settled in. Your father won't be home for a few hours and there are some new young ladies that I must introduce you to."

"Mother?"

He caught her roughly by the arm and she gasped, uncertain of his intentions.

"Yes, Dimi?" she whispered nervously.

"When you introduce me…please use my proper name."

"Of course…Vladimir."

The introductions went as well as could be expected. Vladimir was cordial and cold, but the girls did very poorly in general at concealing their bizarre fascination with him. He could sense their attraction to him; in fact, he could smell it as though they were bitches in heat, and it disgusted him. Really, they were all the same girl anyway. All except one.

Against Nalia's wishes, Sonja cornered Vladimir in the library later that evening.

"You remember me, don't you Dimi? Oh, I mean *Vladimir*," she cooed as she crept up behind him.

"How could I forget you, Sonja?" he replied flatly without looking up from his book.

"Things haven't been the same without you."

"Hmm. I imagine you ladies haven't had anyone to torment since I've been gone."

"Don't say such things. I always loved you," she pouted.

"Ah, yes," he slammed the book shut and met Sonja's eyes with a glare. "You always loved me. I suppose it was in that certain cruel, backstabbing manner in which you girls *love* foolish young men. Or did you mean that you loved me in the carnal sense of the word? You know, that special sort of love that a woman can only give by spreading her legs."

"Well, Dimi, I suppose you have the right to be angry with us," she surrendered playfully. "But we meant no harm. It was just for fun, all the teasing and such—we were just silly little girls, ourselves. What did you expect of us?"

Vladimir laughed. "Not much. I expected nothing other than possibly some compassion or perhaps that you harlots might allow me a little bit of dignity. Oh, and I also expect that you get it into your vicious little mind that my name is Vladimir. You may address me as such, or as Mister Millerovo, or as sir, and that is all. If you call me by that idiotic pet name again, I swear I'll leave a mark."

"Why yes, *sir,*" she sneered and backed away cautiously. "I don't know what it is about you men and your violence. When you don't get your way, you have to destroy everything around you. So, we'll have it your way, *Mister Millerovo*, but in the future please take it under advisement that in this house, men are not to speak to the ladies as though they were common whores." She straightened her hefty body and lifted her head in an attempt to meet Vladimir's height. "Now, I will kindly beg your pardon. I do not wish to quarrel with you any longer. I wouldn't want to end up like Katya, now would I?"

"What exactly do you mean by that? What of Katya?"

"Your mother didn't tell you?"

He shook his head, his eyes blurred with water at the very mention of her name.

"Murdered. Killed by her lover two years ago, now."

Vladimir steadied himself, grasping the writing desk. "Murdered?" he whispered.

"I told her not to leave. She met this man and fell in love, we did not know him. He was from Prague, I think. She ran away with him and one month later, her body was found in a gutter. He'd snapped her neck, but not before beating her bloody. Eighteen years old. I told her not to leave."

"And what of the man?"

Sonja shrugged. "She never told us his name. I only saw him one time, and it was dark, so all I could tell is that he was broad in the shoulders and tall. His hair looked black, but I could be mistaken. It was very dark." She turned to see Vladimir brush a tear from his face. "Well, don't cry about it. She's gone two years now and you hated her anyway. Do you remember your little *collection*? All those dreadful pictures you drew of us? You would have been happy to see her dead back then."

"You've no idea what I wanted back then, nor did you care. Don't waste your breath speculating now."

"Oh, but I do think I know exactly what you wanted, *Mister Millerovo*. And I think Katya and I gave it to you, but you didn't quite know what to do with it. And I think it's made you into a bitter man."

"That's ludicrous. I will not defend my sexual prowess, or lack thereof, based on my performance at the age of thirteen."

"Well, I doubt you've had the opportunity to improve since you've been away at school, unless of course, you've found that boys can be just as comforting as girls. Really, I don't think there's much hope for you at all unless you can stop pining for your mother."

"Do not speak such things about my mother, you wretched beast!"

"You watched her, Vladimir," she laughed maliciously. "You watched her fuck all those men and you pretended it was you she was fucking. We know you did. You did it all the time. I'd wager you still pleasure yourself to the very idea—"

Sonja stopped at once as the back of Vladimir's shaking hand collided with her mouth. He delivered the blow with enough force to make Sonja's sturdy body crash to the floor.

She remained there for a moment, in shock, and then the tears came. She gathered up the massive pile of skirts, rose to her feet with little grace, and tore from the room screaming for Nalia. Vladimir ran after her, uncertain of what to do next, and nearly trampled Marta in the hall.

"What's all this!" Nalia called out amidst the chaos. Sonja had made her way to the parlor, with Marta not far behind. Two other girls found their way to the commotion and were attempting to calm Sonja down.

"He *struck me* in the mouth!" Sonja cried as Nalia pushed her way through the tiny crowd. "Where's Viktor?" she demanded, hysterically. "He *must* know of this!"

"He's not here, Sonja. Now settle yourself and let me see your face," Nalia reached under Sonja's chin, turning her face toward the light of the candelabra. Drops of blood beaded up across the girl's bottom lip and stained her teeth. The skin around her mouth was a deep pink, and black streaks of make-up ran down her otherwise pale face.

"You keep away from me, you *monster*!" Sonja shrieked as Vladimir appeared in the doorway.

"Vladimir," his mother turned to him. "Why did you do this?" Her voice was so gentle.

He could not speak. He stood there, amidst the bewildered she-wolves, shaking and fighting tears.

"Tell her, you fiend," Sonja spat. "Tell her why you would strike me this way."

Still he did not utter a sound. He wished more than anything that he could have replied something simple like *'I struck her because she is a whore,'* but he could say no such thing in the presence of his mother without insulting her character as well. It was a forgivable offence when he was but a confused child, but now it would just be disgraceful. And he certainly could not repeat what Sonja had accused him of. He'd sooner die than suffer such humiliation in front of his mother.

"Go on and tell her, you *snivelling coward*! Tell us all!" Sonja laughed spitefully through her tears.

He wanted so badly to strike her again, to snap her neck the way the Czech had done to Katya. For a moment he could understand how it was that a person could take another's life. Of course, he'd fantasized about it a hundred times, but fantasies were all they'd ever been. But now he could hear Katya taunting and provoking her lover the way she'd done to him as a boy, and the way Sonja was doing to him now. Sonja was a large girl with a thick neck, but Vladimir couldn't imagine her spine being all that much stronger than anyone else's. His hands were powerful enough. Then he felt a hand touch his shoulder with a softness that could only belong to his mother.

"Vladimir…why would you do this?" Nalia asked with tender concern.

His eyes filled with tears and he opened his mouth, but only a small gasp came.

His tears and confusion prompted Nalia to tear up as well.

"Leave us, girls." Nalia cleared her throat and lowered her head. She asked Marta to help Sonja to her quarters, and to assist her with her injury. "I'll join you when I'm finished here."

The girls shuffled from the parlour in silence, even Sonja, who was too angered by the dismissal to speak.

"My son," Nalia whispered tearfully. "Say what you will, but I know you are not well. I can look in your eyes and see *how* you are tormented, but what I cannot see is *why* you are so tortured." She turned away from the young man. "Is it I, Vladimir? Have I done this to you?"

Here it was; he could tell her now. After all, she'd asked, and it was probable that he'd never receive another invitation to confess his truth. He could tell her how the girls had used him and broken him and how he hated them, and how he hated Viktor for keeping them and forcing him to grow up surrounded by them, how he hated Viktor for getting Nalia with child in the first place. He could tell her how he hated all the men she'd let violate her and how he despised her willful ignorance of the whole situation. How could she not realize what she had done to him, how could she be so blind to how much he loved her and wanted to be with her, against her skin, beneath her skin, and inside of her heart and her body? How could she allow him to witness Viktor and those countless other bastards take what should have been his, over and over again? She was sacrosanct to him, but he could do nothing while others desecrated her flesh. Religion and love and hope were dead to him because of the lot of them, yet they did not concern themselves with it. *'Dimi is fine, Dimi is an intelligent boy, Dimi will be just fine.'* But he wasn't. He was dying in his heart and poisoning his body, and still no one thought to stop. Then it was *'Something is wrong with Dimi, Dimi is disturbed, let us send him away.'* No one considered sending away the men or the whores. And that Nalia, an otherwise very intelligent woman, could stand before him now, and with complete sincerity ask him what was wrong, and ask him if it was because of her...she was so beautifully naïve; so absolutely breathtakingly stupid and cruel.

He wanted to scream these things to her; shake her violently. He wanted to be inside her and rip her in half, and he could. Oh, it would be so easy to break the perfectly formed bones in her hips against his thrusting pelvis. It would be nothing for him to crack her ribs with his brutal hands. The vision made him sweat and shake, and his stomach twisted at the onset of arousal, but he held himself as still as he could, breathed in painfully and quietly said, "No, Mother. It isn't you. I...I love you."

"*Oh, Dimi*—forgive me—*Vladimir*. I know this wasn't the most ideal home for you, but it was all we had."

She said it as though he'd grown up in squalor. As he looked around the parlour, with its rich, deep red-and-gold walls and Oriental trimmings, priceless frills and antique furnishings, all velvet and silk, he almost laughed at the irony of her statement.

"But that is why we sent you away to school—because we loved you. We thought it to be the best thing for you."

Vladimir nodded vacantly. "I know this, Mother."

"I am not perfect, Vladimir. I wish I could have been the mother you may have wanted, but this is who I am. This is all I've ever known." She put her arms around her towering son and pressed her face to his chest.

He cautiously returned her embrace and said something he never thought he'd say aloud, especially not to her.

"You were just a child, yourself."

This was the truth, one of the only true things he'd ever said to her. His breath quickened as he realized that this could potentially change their relationship forever. He had been a child, and she had been a child, and now here they were— adults both, together. It was suddenly as though he had never been her son at all. He could just be a man; a man embracing a woman he loves more than life. It was like a dream in that second, where they had no names, no history…just the chemistry and the heat between their bodies.

She lifted her head and gazed up at him, and he could feel her heart beating heavily against his torso; he could see the pulse in her neck grow faster and deeper. He could kiss her, the way he'd always desired, because now she desired it too.

But then her forehead creased in confusion, so quickly, he barely had time to stop himself.

"What did you say to me?"

He felt his throat constrict and pulled back slightly. "I said you were just a child, yourself…when you had me."

The most insincere smile Vladimir had ever seen slid across her alabaster face and she said, "Vladimir, what a ridiculous thing to say! I was hardly a child—I was fifteen years old!"

I left my parents house that evening, before Viktor returned and before my mother could have a chance to think about what I'd said and what I'd nearly done. I'd obviously gone mad~ as I write this now, almost three decades after the fact, I cannot fathom what possessed me. None the less, there was nothing left for me in that house. What good could come of my presence, after all? The courtesans were terrified of me, and I despised them so. It would be years before I would attempt to return, and even then, I never made it to their door. I lied to your mother, telling her I had seen them and that they did not approve of our union, but none of it was true. I merely wanted to keep those terrible memories at bay, away from your mother, and ultimately away from you. But now here I am, confessing things to you that I have been utterly afraid to even think, let alone say. I half wish you to burn this journal before you are burdened any further.

Moscow, 1857

And off to University he went, lost and broken and quietly deranged. He hid it well enough at first. To his professors he seemed just another poorly socialized and intensely serious pupil, overwhelmed by too many books and theories, and intimidated to the point of absolute terror by the accomplishments and the stern faces of his mentors. It was an amazing time to operate within the realm of science and medicine. It seemed as though at any moment a brand new era would emerge, and Moscow was poised to be at the forefront.

Vladimir immersed himself in his studies. Really, it was all he could do given the way things had unravelled at home. It seemed a promising solution at first; Vladimir rarely drank during his first semester, nor did he crave any sort of intoxicant. During this brief period of sobriety he began to rekindle his love affair with knowledge.

In his scholarly mania, Vladimir began to teach himself other languages, as many of them as he could manage between his other studies. As a young child, Nalia had taught him to speak French and English, which he could still do moderately well, although not fluently. He was a remarkably quick learner, but because of his 'emotional distractions and shortcomings'—as one professor would call it—his capacity for learning was not what it could have been. His professors maintained that discipline would be Vladimir's only salvation, but Vladimir disagreed. He was saved, little by little, whenever he would come to discover something new. It could be a formula, or an understanding of another culture in the course of learning a language; really, it was the feeling of discovery that kept him alive.

By the start of his sophomore year, Vladimir began to crawl out of his fortress of isolation, books and papers, yearning for other curious souls with which to share his knowledge. Of course, his fellow pupils and professors were able to engage him in the occasional interesting conversation, but those sessions were always so formal and staid, with no place for personality or adventurous speculation. He longed to find himself amidst the pioneers, the Sechenovs and the Pavlovs. Vladimir was in awe of the school of thought that seemed to unify physiology and behaviour. To talk of thoughts and emotions and the intangible elements of the brain and psyche, as well as hard science and chemicals in the same forum was an incredible thing. Vladimir felt a stirring deep within him at the very idea of one day working with his idols.

It was during that year that Vladimir happened across the works of an intriguing scientist who he'd not yet encountered in his prior studies. In fact, it would be two or three more years before this scientist would find his way into the Russian curriculum but in the meantime, Vladimir spent hours of his own time familiarizing himself with the enthralling theories of the evolutionist called Charles Darwin.

And that was my life until sometime in 1861, at which time I suffered another emotional collapse, due to my demons and ~I sadly must admit to you~ my lapse into near constant inebriation. I had not spoken to my mother since that disastrous evening many years before, nor had I exchanged words with Viktor in ages, but I found myself in enough distress to write them a letter telling them how I would be leaving school for an undetermined period of time. I've never told anyone where I went in that time, but I shall tell you now~ I set off for England. I don't recall my intentions when I made that decision, but it was on that journey that I first visited the sight of your future home. Of course, at that time I was not looking to purchase land, nor did I have the means to do such a thing, but I remember as I was travelling through the countryside.

<hr />

"*God,* how I remember it *so* clearly," Vladimir choked back long overdue tears and hid his face in his hands. He was alone now in his dirty London flat, speaking to no one but himself. He'd sent young Mary back out to the streets, back to Pinkney, back to the lions. He couldn't save her, and they both knew it. He promised he'd ask for her again, but there would be no guarantee she'd return. There would be no keeping her safe from rapists and lunatics and wolves in the interim, but the poor child would have been no safer had she stayed with him. Veda was dead because of him, he turned his back on his mother, he'd failed to save Katya from the treacherous streets, and he couldn't save himself from anything at all. And failing Anastacia…that had been the deepest, most shameful act he'd ever committed.

He closed his eyes, his dark lids weighted with guilt, but it was only a moment before the thick darkness faded to grey, and then to green. Grey and green, that was the England he remembered; an entirely different England than the one he lived in now. London was a city, like all cities— diseased and cluttered. It was not even in the same world as the lands to the north. It was peaceful there, and it was *open*. Not *open* in the vast, empty, cold grey manner of Russia, but open and *free*. The grey in Lancashire wasn't cold, it was smouldering charcoal poured across velvet and silken greens. It was slate and earth, stone relics and clear streams. It was where he wanted to die and be buried. And now, with that prospect just beyond his shadow, he knew his soul would never rest until his daughter was living a peaceful life in that same beautifully green land.

Moscow 1862

After several months of rest and rejuvenation, Vladimir returned to Moscow, hoping to pick up where he left off— a goal that would quickly prove to be unrealistic. He had run away at a terribly crucial period in his academic career, allowing his colleagues to advance in their training and subsequently damaging his chances to find opportunities within the upper echelon of research.

It required a great deal of effort to convince his superiors that he would be worth their time; they had seen his kind before, unstable addicts from wealthy families who used their money to coerce people into tolerating their incompetence, thus accepting them as productive members of society. Certainly, Vladimir was intelligent, but he was also presumed useless by most.

Relations with his fellow students were just as feeble. After his 'sabbatical', no one really took him seriously, and he was subject to much ridicule and slander throughout the campus. At best, those peers who didn't have time for such petty derision ignored him like the tall, sickly ghost he was. He did not socialize outside of school, and he tended to avoid women and functions that might include women whenever possible. He might have spent the rest of his days at university completely alone if it hadn't been for Ivo.

Ivan Kursk, called 'Ivo' by some, was—by Vladimir's definition—a kindred spirit of sorts. He seemed to be a solitary soul, the kind of romantic character that held an air of mystery and tragedy. He always wore a coat and cap of black wool, and had eyes and hair to match. He was a very intense looking young man, with remarkably sharp features and a dark shadow of hair across his stern jaw. He might have intimidated Vladimir if he'd been taller, but as it was, Vladimir had the advantage, a trivial fact that had become a thorn in his side ever since one of the students caustically remarked to another that Vladimir's height was the *only* quality that put him above anyone else at school.

Vladimir first noticed the young stranger at the library; rather, he noticed the young stranger noticing him. Kursk wasted no time once eye contact was made, and he casually approached Vladimir as though they'd known each other for years.

"Millerovo, that is your name, yes?"

Vladimir nodded.

"Do you know who I am?"

"I do not."

"I did not expect that you would. I doubt you know half as much about me as I know about you."

"I don't believe I know anything about you, sir." Vladimir gradually came to realize that this man was making him uncomfortable, yet his curiosity would force him to carry on with the conversation.

"Kursk."

"I beg your pardon?"

"Ivan Kursk. That is my name. My friends call me Ivo."

"Why is that?"

The man grinned, snarled really, his face suggesting both amusement and disgust. "My father's name is Ivan, and I am *nothing* like my father."

"*That,* I can understand. I would like to think that I am nothing like my father, either."

"You are the son of Viktor Millerovo the second, yes?"

"How do you know this?" Vladimir palms suddenly felt wet, and his mouth was going dry.

"You are infamous in certain circles, man. You did not know this?"

Vladimir shook his head and swallowed hard.

"Vladimir Millerovo, son of Viktor, raised in a house of ill-repute, surrounded by that rare breed of loose and intelligent woman which, for some enigmatic reason, left him extremely well rounded, well learned, and utterly mad." Ivo smiled again; a wicked gleam in his eyes. "Presently, he secretly enjoys massive quantities of vodka, mind-altering substances, reading Charles Darwin, and is charmingly nervous, or possibly nervously charming, I have yet to decide which. Have I forgotten anything significant?"

He wanted to run away from this man. In a single moment, he both hated and loved him. He questioned the man's sexuality, and for a second he questioned his own. He felt a chemistry quite unlike anything he'd ever experienced before, but he quickly found himself feeling sick at the very thought. His mind whirled in circles and he considered hitting the man as easily as he could consider kissing him on the mouth. And in less than two seconds, these thoughts were created and silently released into the space between them, and into the world.

He meant to ask how he knew all of this, but all he said was, "No. I don't believe you missed much at all."

"Well, don't concern yourself with it. I come from my father's filthy money, I drink too much, and I'm a complete bastard, so I think we have much in common."

Ivo's smile became a quiet laugh, inciting Vladimir to do the same, in spite of his confusion.

"I know a place we can go and have a drink." Ivo placed his hand on Vladimir's shoulder. "Come on, friend."

It was the first time in his life he'd been called 'friend'.

Ivo's home reminded Vladimir of the one in which he'd been raised: large and ornate, with a warmth that could imply either comfort or debauchery. This house, however, showed signs of misuse and neglect. There was a deep layer of dust on every surface and the stale odour of smoke lingered heavily in the air. There were crystal glasses and empty carafes toppled over and strewn about, spilling liquid and cigarette ashes onto polished veneers and valuable Persian carpets. He motioned Vladimir to have a seat and poured two drinks.

"Is this your family's home?"

Ivo lit a rolled cigarette and offered one to Vladimir, which he accepted more out of courtesy than craving.

"No, it's all mine, and although I *should* be, I'm not ashamed to say I purchased it with my father's money, along with all of the terribly expensive art and furnishings that I don't actually give a damn about. I merely wanted to abuse his shallow generosity. If I could, I'd dry him out, but I think he may be on to my game. He's a bit more reserved with my allowance these days."

"So, what did your father do to you?" Vladimir could hardly believe that he'd been so presumptuous as to ask this stranger such a personal question. He would have been offended if someone did so to him, but he was presently under the impression that standard rules of etiquette did not apply around Ivo.

"My *father...*" Ivo took a long, deep drag of his cigarette, then let the smoke pour from his mouth and nose in a thick milky stream. "My father is the only man I've ever met who is more of a bastard than I, only he doesn't possess half my wit or intellect. All of the arrogance, none of the personality," he grinned and reached for his drink, his hand blindly crawling across the wasteland of debris on the tabletop in search of the glass. "My father, Ivan the Second, Ivan the Terrible, Ivan the Imperious Imperialist. Men like my father created a world in which money keeps the ignorant securely stationed above the learned or creative, where they can be watched and controlled. We wouldn't want someone with any sort of vision stepping in and prying open the encrusted eyes of the masses, now would we? Men like my father are so busy throwing their money and utterly misinformed ideals around, that they haven't a clue of what lies in store—not just for this country, but for all of society. They've been so busy with their self-congratulatory orgies that they've yet to notice how close their *world* is to complete annihilation."

Vladimir nodded, although he still did not quite understand Ivo's answer. Had the senior Ivan beaten his son, or degraded him in some way? Had he disgraced the honour of his family by living an immoral life, committed rape or murder? What was it, exactly, that this man had done to earn such contempt from his child? Had he done more than take a political stance that differed from his son's? But Vladimir did not ask these questions aloud. He would not attempt to engage his new friend in an emotionally dangerous game of 'who has suffered the greater misfortune', though Vladimir would have wagered his entire inheritance that Ivo would lose.

"And what of your upbringing?" Ivo asked in an amused tone. "Tell me how it was to come of age in one of Moscow's most notorious and revered brothels."

Vladimir cleared his throat and curled his shaking hands into tight fists. "It was…" he frantically searched for an appropriate word, one word that could describe his home, if that was even possible. Treacherous, agonizing, hellish, chaotic: these words came to mind, but to avoid yet another emotional outburst he would keep his answer as vague as he could. "It was…unusual." It was the truest false answer he could give.

"Unusual?" Ivo smirked. "Well, I'd imagine so."

Vladimir shrugged and gazed vacantly at the smoke from his cigarette as it lazily drifted by. He watched as the ashes fell to his lap and thought how he might like to do the very same one of these days, just burn from the inside out and collapse into a worthless pile of ash. No resurrecting embers, no Phoenix to speak of…just a fine, grey powder. Just dust.

Ivo turned out to be a persistent fellow, tracking Vladimir down night after night and luring him to his home with the promise of intoxicants and stimulating conversation. Ivo shared Vladimir's fascination with Darwin, though he approached it from a very different angle than Vladimir. He spoke of a societal application to survival of the fittest, in which the most intelligent and cunning advance and the ignorant face a slow extinction, which seemed not at all scientific to Vladimir, but intriguing none the less. Of course, between the drink and the opium, a conversation about the dust on the mantle could have enthralled them for hours at a time. Not surprisingly, Vladimir's schoolwork began to suffer again, although he was not too harshly chastised by the professors who had essentially given up on him. The few instructors who still held onto a glimmer of hope that the young Millerovo boy might prove to be worth the effort lectured him daily on responsibility, commitment, and the merits of advancement.

"Advancement! *Ha!*" Ivo quipped when Vladimir recounted the speech he'd heard often enough to commit to memory. "That's *brilliant*. 'Study harder Mister Millerovo, and you just might acquire all the bloody *advancement* you could dare desire!'" He mocked in a singsong voice. "Did they happen to mention that the more you learn, the more of a threat you'll become to the current social structure? Unless, of course, you intend to keep your head low, your mouth shut, and glide on your family's wealth to a position at the top of the scientific food chain, like the vast majority have done for years."

Vladimir's head was swimming and the sweet smoke of opium burned his eyes. All those words...my, how Ivo could fit so many words in the spaces between breaths. But Vladimir did not mind this. He could feel no pain.

"I do not intend to use my father's money for any sort of advancement. Travel to exotic locales, and opium, certainly. But advancement? *Never*." Vladimir grinned. It had been a long time since a grin happened naturally.

"Good," Ivo smiled. "Carry on with that sort of talk and they'll never see it coming."

"See what coming?"

"Change, my dear man—as a result of revolution."

～

I knew from the beginning that Ivo and I were profoundly different animals, but my yearning for companionship outweighed my better judgement, and I allowed myself to fall under his spell. Ivo saw me for exactly what I was~ a weak and desperate man that could be easily seduced, a lonely outcast to do his bidding in exchange for company and a false sense of importance. And I saw Ivo for exactly what he was~ not a revolutionary as he would have had the world believe, but a spoiled aristocrat, bored with the gilded life he'd been handed. Ivo Kursk was an opium addict, and truly not much more. Certainly he was a handsome one, with a quick wit and sharp tongue, but despite his intelligence, he held no understanding whatsoever of what an anarchistic state would be like in reality. He would have easily been one of the first to fall.

I am certain that you of all people know the pain that comes with feeling alone, and I pray that you might understand why I went along with Kursk and his plans. You see, my darling, Ivo's idea was to use me in order to alter the minds of men. He was searching for the means to create something he called 'Chemical Evolution'.

I have never been the most rational man ~as I have proved to you time and time again~ and I would have done almost anything to ensure a place in his life, and since Ivo was obsessed with finding a way to 'evolve' as a means to change society one mind at a time, so he claimed~ though I knew it to be nothing more than the search for a cure to his ennui~ I had to become equally as enthralled. I was the alchemist, and he was my King. I nearly loved him, Ana. I wish I'd been a stronger man.

～

"Do you understand what I'm saying, Vladimir? I'm speaking of a drug—something much stronger than the likes of this." Ivo shook his pipe in the air. "I want something to help us *see*. I mean, *really see* what lies before us, around us—what lies in the minds of the oppressors. Do you understand this?"

"You want me to create a drug that will allow you to read another's thoughts."

"You make it sound silly, but, yes. But not only that—a drug that forces the blinders from your eyes, a drug that can be given to the masses in order to help them evolve—or *advance*, as your professors would say."

"So they can rise up and change society."

"Exactly!"

"But before a change can occur in reality, it must occur in the mind."

"Yes, yes, *yes*…I knew you'd understand!" In his excitement, he grabbed Vladimir by the back of his neck and kissed him, forcefully and quickly on the mouth.

Vladimir sat back, slightly stunned, but mostly drunk and bewildered. "Yes… yes I do understand," he replied. "I understand that you are completely mad."

"*Mad*? How can you say such a thing? It's a brilliant idea."

"Well, it's certainly a creative idea. Unfortunately, it has absolutely no basis in the world of science. You are asking me to manufacture witchcraft."

"No, not witchcraft."

"Perhaps you should go into town, seek out a gypsy fortune teller and ask her to sell you a magic potion. I'm certain they peddle such things, along with magic rocks and talismans."

"Am I sensing sarcasm, Vladimir?"

"My apologies," Vladimir rubbed his eyes and grinned.

"I thought you of all people would be up for the challenge, but if not, then I have no doubt I can find another chemist. Perhaps someone with a bit more vision."

Oh, yes—that's right, that's just like you—you who are no better than the whores I used to know, the blue-blooded whores that used me as a pawn in their cruel parlour games. What can we take from Dimi, what can we bleed out of him before we cast him aside like a like a broken trinket? What do you want to take from Dimi, dear Ivo...dear Ivan? Make haste and take it now, before he's all used up. Take it now before he disappears...before I am barren...

And Vladimir sat still in that unending moment, gazing into the space between Ivo and himself, wounded and silent. *What of friendship? What of brotherhood? Do these things crumble so easily under the weight of expectation?*

But Vladimir, being who he was, did not question Ivo. He simply said, "No. Do not seek the aid of another. I will help you."

⌁

I spent the next four years of my life dividing my time and energy between school and Ivo, who was the only reason I remained at the university at all. I would have certainly and rightly been expelled for my excessive absences and erratic performance, had it not been for my friend, who persuaded the board to look the other way with a large sum of his father's money, allowing me to continue my studies. Ivo detested this contribution, but I needed certain resources in order to carry out his idea, the most vital being knowledge.

While I was most appreciative of such an opportunity, and Ivo's generosity, I must truthfully confess that I had no firm understanding of what he thought he was going to accomplish, nor did I have any idea of where to begin. It seemed more like a task for a wizard or an alchemist, rather than an ordinary chemist, but I did what I could in earnest, and the more time I spent with Ivo, the more I began to believe that his fantastic dream might actually become a reality.

⌁

Of course, Vladimir had no way to predict what events would unfold as a result of his partnership with Ivo. Imagine how it would be to glimpse each consecutive link in the chain of experiences that make the sum of a life with each decision, and to see all possible paths that lead from every one of those links. It would be difficult to pinpoint the exact link at which Vladimir's life began to fall to pieces, as he could have chosen a different path at any juncture. It is unlikely that he would have chosen the fate that he did, for in his heart Vladimir was not an evil man, he simply chose to walk treacherous paths.

～≋～

He was daydreaming over heavy books and a nearly empty flask, walking through the green and grey forests of Lancashire, listening to the rustling of fox in the underbrush and the faint sounds of water rushing over small stones in the nearby stream. The riverbed was black with sediment, and the water so clear that from the hills above it resembled a long black snake, slithering around the trees and through the rocky valley. He remembered the farm that lay alongside the stream, with its unreal green grasses and ancient stone walls, but mostly he remembered the steep slate cliffs at the place where the stream narrowed into a shallow creek, and turned more rock than water. The water trickled down to the bottom of the deep ravine, becoming silent and afraid in the shadow of its high cliff walls. Vladimir thought how good it would be to die there; swallowed by the warm, black peat and marked by the smooth, perfect stone.

He dreamed so much these days. Ivo was relentless in his quest for evolution, which really meant that Vladimir would get no peace until it was done, so in the interim, Vladimir would dream.

Nightly, Ivo would come to Vladimir's decrepit apartment—rented with the stipend that Ivo provided him—to check on the progress and, of course, to engage in their vices of choice. And nightly, Vladimir would listen to his companion complain about the room that he'd rented.

"Why—with the more than adequate amount of money I've given you—would you choose a place like…this?"

"I do not see the point in wasting your money on an extravagant apartment, when I could be using it for our cause."

"And which cause would that be? The one we're drinking, or the one we're smoking?" Ivo laughed.

"The cause that keeps me up all hours of the night and causes my work at university to suffer so dreadfully. Oh, and also the cause that prevents me from having any sort of social life other than getting drunk with you."

"I resent that, my friend. You stay up all hours because you are a hopeless insomniac and you needn't concern yourself with your school assignments, since I've ensured that you'll graduate with all the proper papers regardless of your marks. And do not dare to pretend that you'd be out and about, cavorting with some stunningly beautiful and intelligent, well-bred woman that has a penchant for drunken, neurotic scientists-in-training that live in run-down flats in the slums of Moscow, if only it weren't for me and my oppressive expectations."

"Allow me my dreams, Ivo," Vladimir chuckled as he knocked over the flask.

"When this is done, my dear man, the dreams you have now will pale in comparison."

The research took its toll on me, as it had in the past, and eventually I succumbed to the pressures. I feared I was losing my mind, having spent most days and nights sequestered in my tight, dimly lit room, surrounded by books and the makings of a rudimentary laboratory~ the components of which I had smuggled from the university lab. I often wondered if Ivo's bribe would have spared me from prosecution had I been discovered, but soon enough I would come to realize that the threat of punishment from the university would be the very least of my worries.

But as it was, I turned my thoughts from anything that hinted at consequence and pressed on in hopes of discovering Ivo's magic potion. My rationale was this: within the brain there are channels, deep creases and ravines ~you see, I'd been thinking of the ravine in Lancashire again~ and within these ravines are chemicals and these chemicals set off minuscule reactions which seem to trigger different parts of the mind~ emotions, memories, behaviours, perceptions, and so on. It seemed plausible to me that if those chemicals were strengthened, then it would directly affect the mind's abilities, make them stronger as well. It seems rather simple as I tell it now, but it took hundreds of hours before everything began to fall into place. I will not bore you with formulas here, even if I could remember them. But it was a fool's errand, and in the end I was not successful, but I came so very close to...something. What? I do not know, but it was something unusual. Something special. I created a drug that had temporary effects on perception, but I had no way of determining what was real and what was mere hallucination, and that would not do. It was not enough. I do not know if my research will ever see the light of day again, as it was left behind ~in haste~ in the custody of Étienne. God knows what has become of it all, or if it is better off lost for all eternity. Perhaps what I discovered in my quest is not something that any human should carry any farther. Perhaps I am guilty of treading on god's territory and our awful fate has been the price for such a crime. I do not know these things, but what I believe is that I possibly came very close to realizing Ivo's dream of accelerated evolution. I nearly discovered the key to becoming god-like.

⮞

It was in the spring of 1866 that Vladimir completed his courses at university, albeit several terms behind his class, and only by the merciful greed of the university board. He was exhausted and frayed and still nowhere near a viable solution to Ivo's plan, but Ivo—not being completely soulless—took pity on his fragile chemist and suggested that he use a portion of the project funds to take a holiday.

"I do not care where you go. Just come back clear-headed and ready to work," Ivo instructed. "And Vladimir…do not speak of our project to anyone. Perhaps I do not need to say it, but I will sleep better at night knowing that I did."

In June of 1866, Vladimir set off for a small town in Romania, on the coast of the Black Sea. It was a beautiful, peaceful place called Constanta.

~

Veda had grown accustomed to being without Vladimir for numerous reasons. Upon their return to Moscow, Vladimir spent much of his time working with a man that Veda had met very briefly in the first month after her arrival. This would be the first of a very few meetings, although she felt as if her husband's *friend* shared every aspect of their lives by proxy. All she ever heard from Vladimir was, "I must meet with Ivo," or "Ivo needs me to stay with him this evening if we are to get anything accomplished."

Ivo seemed to have a great deal of influence over Vladimir, which struck her as odd since Vladimir had not once muttered the name Ivan Kursk when they were in Constanta. It was only once they were in Moscow that she knew such a man even existed.

But Ivo was everywhere, dictating their every move from the very beginning. It was at his command that Vladimir moved his laboratory from the tiny apartment and into the attic of Ivo's house. Veda was grateful for the extra space, but would have gladly traded it to have Vladimir working at home by her side. And it was because of Ivo that her husband stayed away many nights 'slaving away' at their project, of which she still knew nothing. And it was because of Ivo that her husband would stumble home at daybreak reeking of perspiration and liquor.

In the beginning, on the other side of town, the good side of town, Ivo repeatedly expressed his displeasure at Vladimir's new situation.

"How is it that I send you off on holiday to relax and clear your head—essentially simplify your life—and you return home with nothing but complication and clutter?"

"Are you calling my wife *clutter*?"

"No, Vladimir. Your wife is a lovely woman," Ivo sneered. "I'm saying that your situation, *your life*, is now more complicated and cluttered. Think about it, man! This project has demanded all of your time and energy and will continue to do so. Did you ever *once* consider that a woman would also demand all of your time and energy?"

"Veda understands that I must work. She's not one to fuss after me about things that are necessary."

"Yes, but your work does not understand that you now must divide your time. It will not carry on of its own accord!"

"Is it my work that does not understand, Ivo, or is it you?"

Ivo rubbed his face and sighed. "This discussion is futile." He lowered his head in defeat.

"Ivo, please…we can make this work. I know we can…"

"Do you intend to leave your wife?" Ivo snapped.

Vladimir shook his head. "Of course not."

"Then there is nothing more for me to say. I will have to make do with having you only part of the time, even if the work suffers for it."

"It will not suffer. I will not disappoint you, my friend. I can still call you that, can't I?"

Ivo met him squarely in the eyes. "I suppose time shall tell."

Vladimir tried his very best to give equal time to his two priorities, but it soon proved to be more than he could manage. If only he did not have to sleep. It burned him to no end that so many hours were wasted on it. He did not intend for things to work out as they did, but he could think of no other solutions, and soon the only moments spent with Veda were the mostly unsatisfying ones that occurred in their bed.

Life continued in this manner for nearly another full year until just before Veda became pregnant. It was only then that Vladimir began to wean himself from Ivo and the project and pay a bit more mind to his lonely wife after she threatened to leave him and return to Constanta.

Vladimir was being pulled taut from both sides; if he committed to the project he would lose his wife, and if he committed to his wife, he'd lose the work, and the money, and most likely their home, meagre as it was. Even worse, he'd lose Ivo.

But on the day that Veda told him the news, the decision was made for him. He was to be a father, and damn his own soul to hell should he be as negligent as his father was to him. And at Veda's request, it was on that day that he vowed to drink no more.

He went to Ivo to regretfully admit that his mate had been correct. A choice had to be made, after all. Ivo sat before him, his face like stone as Vladimir nervously explained his reasons for leaving and, in turn, offered suggestions for the sake of the project. Ivo would have to understand that Vladimir needed to find steady, legal work that paid well enough to support his family while still affording him time to care for his wife and unborn child. He could not risk their well-being by committing further crimes the way they'd done from the start. He pleaded with Ivo to accept this, and to allow him some time to find work before cutting off funds. Winter was quickly approaching and he feared eviction if Ivo refused to pay at least one more month's rent. Ivo could scarcely believe the audacity of his colleague.

"Amazing. You come to me crying, *'To hell with your dreams, Ivo. Like a short-sighted idiot I've impregnated a gypsy woman and can no longer deal with you. We must simply disregard all the energy and time and money we've invested in this project and move on. And by the way, would you be so kind as to continue to pay me until I can find something better?'* Utterly amazing."

"Ivo, please. That's not what I mean to say at all. I have nothing but respect for your ideas and love for you. As a friend, I am coming to you for understanding and assistance. I humbly ask for your help. Please do not misunderstand my words…"

"Respect and love—understanding, friendship, and humility. That's quite a positive picture you've painted there, *my friend*. But I must *humbly* ask for your *forgiveness* if I feel as though you do not *understand* what it is to *respect and love*."

"Ivo, I am so very sorry…I…"

Ivo raised his hand to silence Vladimir and walked to the door. "Say no more, please. I've been anticipating this day ever since you returned to me with that wanton beggar woman on your arm. Therefore, I have had time to consider what I would do when you finally abandoned me, and quite fortunately for you and your impending family I have decided to be the bigger man and save you one last time from the poverty and misery which will undoubtedly befall you in time. You have one month, then you are on your own and I request in return that you never again utter my name or show your pallid face at my door."

How it pained me to walk away from him. At the time I did not even care about the work. I left all of the research, all of the chemicals, everything, in his attic. And with him, I left a piece of myself. I could tell Veda very little of this, for she would never have understood. I could not tell her of the project, and I could not have explained to her my relationship to Ivo. There were times when I thought she suspected we might be lovers, but we never were ~at the very least, not physically. But I did love him, or feel something much like love for him, and I could not help but to think that he may have felt the same. It was in silent moments, when the talking ceased and our eyes would search the room, perhaps looking for some kind of understanding or reason for the electricity

that filled the air between us. It was in the way I thought about him incessantly when he was not near. Taking a holiday seemed like torture at first, because he was not with me, although I eventually succumbed to the distraction that was your mother. And I will confess that I thought of him on that holiday when I was alone in my room, in the bed that he paid for, in ways that are not natural, and I confess that I responded to those thoughts in kind. It happened twice, and each time I'd been drinking, but I shall not make excuses for my behaviours because while I did not again indulge in that sort of physical pleasuring, I did think of him many times thereafter while I was sober and with Veda. But it was ultimately in the way he had said in his final words that day, "I have anticipated this day ever since you returned to me with that wanton beggar woman on your arm." He said 'returned to me', not 'since you came back' or 'came home', but 'returned to me'. Perhaps I am reading too much into his choice of words, but my heart tells me the truth.

So for eight months I remained sober and severed from Ivo. I worked myriad jobs, all of which were far beneath my level of qualification, some of which were not even in my field, but I did whatever I had to do to keep us fed and warm and sane.

You must be asking why I did not turn to our families in such desperate times ~and I shall tell you. While Veda's family was not poor, they had very little money. But you have to understand that in their culture, they had little need for money. Veda's father and brothers provided food and shelter with their own hands, her mother provided clothing and her grandmother tended to the livestock and gardens.

My family...well, I considered paying them a visit, but my pride and resentfulness held me back. Truly, I could not use the money earned from the flesh of one child to care for another.

Your mother and I never raised our voices to each other over financial matters, but our little home was filled to the brim with tension and worry throughout her pregnancy. I feared for her health and yours, but Veda was strong and brought you through the freezing winter. Regrettably, I was not so strong and by the end of her term, I would crumble under the weight of my greatest weakness.

Moscow 1869

There was no more money. There was no more work. Vladimir, with his erratic behaviour and nervous ways, was dismissed from yet another job. Of course, he was not fired from each and every one, but there was always a reason that the work was not suited to him. Sometimes this would prompt him to leave, and sometimes his condescending attitude would prompt his employers to ask him to leave. He wanted to believe that he deserved better, but beneath everything, he knew it wasn't true.

Veda, on the other hand, truly did deserve better. She was due any day and Vladimir had still made no arrangements for a midwife. He failed to mention this to Veda, who was under the impression that her husband had taken care of things, just they way he said. She was expecting the midwife to come calling at any time, and would feel much better once she arrived.

But there was no midwife anywhere in sight when Veda's water broke on that blustery day. Vladimir was gone as well and Veda suddenly realized that she knew nothing of his whereabouts. She was utterly alone, and going into labour a million miles away from her family, cut off from Vladimir's parents, without friends and, on that day, without her husband. The cramping in her pelvis was great enough to impair her ability to walk and left her with no other choice than to crawl across the floor and slowly make her way down the stairs, backwards and on all fours, to the stranger's apartment below, leaving a trail of blood and fluid as she went.

As his wife pounded on the neighbour's door, frightened and calling for help in a tongue not understood by the old woman inside, Vladimir stood meekly on the front stairs of a familiar home and knocked on the door of Ivan Kursk.

The small wrinkled woman who lived on the floor beneath the Millerovo's recognized the distress in Veda's voice and quickly beckoned her visiting grandson to assist the pregnant woman inside. Veda searched for the correct words, eventually conveying to the pair that she did not know where her husband was, and that the midwife he'd promised her never came. She had no doctor, no family to turn to.

She could not understand much of what was being said; they spoke so quickly, quite unlike the way Vladimir spoke to her. To an outsider, his method of communication with his wife might have seemed condescending, as though he was speaking to a child, but it was the only way Veda could learn the language. For this reason, Veda had very few opportunities to socialise, although she would never wish to burden her husband with complaints. He had too many troubles and did not need such petty things heaped upon him. But as it was, her silence led her to this place of confusion and fear and now she would give birth in a strange place with no loved ones to hold her hand, and would very soon have to bid all modesty farewell in the presence of—

She did not even know their names.

While the old woman fussed around her head, gently mumbling words that Veda assumed to be expressions of comfort, the grandson, who could not have been much older than Veda, readied the bed for delivery. If she could have understood him, she'd have known that he was very sorry for any embarrassment to come and that he was ready to do his very best despite his complete lack of experience in midwifery.

"Is this how you repay me?" Ivo stared at Vladimir in disbelief. "I give you money, I tie up all of your loose ends, and ask only one thing in return—that you should stay away from me—and now here you stand, not even a full year later, cluttering up my doorway with your oppressive quandaries and pathetic demeanour."

But Vladimir, no stranger to abuse, held his tongue, lowered his head, and simply said, "Ivo, I've made a mistake."

"Oh, what's this now? Could you be saying I was correct about our little *situation*?" Ivo grinned maliciously. "Though perhaps I should be the bigger man here and not rub salt into your self-inflicted wounds," he paused, "but then again, I might enjoy a few delicious, albeit predictable, moments of discomfort at your expense. I think I am owed that, at the least. So go on then, speak your piece, and make sure I can hear the desperation clearly."

And for every word of regret and humility uttered by Vladimir came an equally painful ear-splitting scream from his young wife as she delivered their daughter into the arms of a complete stranger.

After doing every humiliating thing short of standing on his head while singing praises to his former partner, Vladimir finally persuaded Ivo to take him back into the fold. He'd even broken his promise to Veda and had a celebratory drink with his companion. In fact, he had several celebratory drinks throughout the evening, which could only be appropriately finished off with a dose of laudanum.

And so, everyone was happy again. Vladimir would again have money enough to put food on the table, and of course, he'd have Ivo again, and Ivo had Vladimir in the palm of his hand. Whatever Ivo wanted, he would get now that Vladimir was eternally indebted to him. The project would be resurrected and all would be right with the world.

The sun was creeping its way through the morning clouds as Vladimir staggered through the streets, still reeking of sweet smoke and musk and completely unprepared for what awaited him at home.

The world is surreal today, he thought. The weight of worry he'd carried these last nine months was gone, only to be replaced with what felt like a gnawing rodent inside his gut, but that was a sensation he would deal with later. For now, he would simply try to enjoy the feeling of euphoria before it faded away.

And the street was quiet, and the vagrant in the stairwell was gone, and the air around him smelled of impending spring instead of trash and cold piss. He was so taken with these changes that he did not immediately notice the viscous trail that led from the neighbour's door to his own.

Veda was not in their room. He stood dumbfounded for several minutes, trying to imagine where it was that his very pregnant wife would have gone. His heart sank as he looked to the floor and saw the large stain beneath his feet.

"*Veda!* Where are you?" he cried frantically, following the trail of blood down the stairs. "*Veda, oh god*, where are you?"

The trail stopped at the door one level down, but before he could knock, the old woman opened it and beckoned him inside.

Veda was on the bed—a stranger's bed—her eyes half closed and her hair slicked against her face in bizarre swirls and coils, and beside her, the tiniest creature Vladimir had ever seen was suckling at her breast.

Tears came to his eyes and he approached the bed with great caution, as though Veda were a wild fox protecting her young.

"Veda?"

Veda did not move except to shift her bloodshot eyes toward her husband. They were full of poison and Vladimir could feel it burn through his skin as he came closer still.

"You were not here." Her voice was low and tired, nearly a soft growl.

"I know, my love, I cannot express my sorrow or my anger with myself…"

"You did not send for a midwife."

94

"Oh, Veda, my love…please forgive me. I haven't the words…"

Veda cast her eyes back to the child, and in an instant, they were full of love again.

Vladimir swallowed hard and reached out to brush Veda's hair from her cheek. "I wish to hold our child. Please let me see."

"You may hold her once you are sober and do not stink of betrayal."

"Hold *her*…" He pulled his hand away and tucked it between his knees. "I have a daughter," he whispered, tears still falling. Veda did not know if it was a statement or a question.

The elderly woman suggested that Vladimir clean himself up and come back later. He stared at her, realizing that in all the time he lived in the building, he never bothered to know the woman's name. He looked to the young man who sat quietly in the corner, his shirt stained with blood.

"I cannot thank you enough. You saved my wife and child and I will forever be indebted to you."

"You can repay us by going upstairs and pulling yourself together so when you return it will be as a decent father and husband," the young man said calmly.

Vladimir was taken aback by the boy's boldness, but held his tongue, knowing that the young man spoke the truth.

"What is your name, young man?"

"Josef. My grandmother is called Ana."

"It is for Anastacia," the old woman added.

"That's a lovely name."

"I'm glad you feel that way," Veda said, coldly. "It is the name I've given to our daughter."

Although she said nothing more about my despicable behaviour that day, having far more important things to attend, I knew a seed of irreconcilable disgust had been

planted. There would be a long period of cultivation before that seed became a gar-den of hatred, but none the less, I ruined everything with my lack of self-control and foresight that spring, just as I knew I would. At least I am, if nothing else, predictable.

But you…you she loved more and more with each passing second. I could see her in your beautifully thick hair, your plump little mouth, and your Black Sea eyes; and in your perfect little nose and delicate hands, in your smooth alabaster skin, I saw my own mother. Please do not take offence, I do not mean to compare you to the woman I have described in a most indecent light, but my mother as she was in the first light of morning ~sans the layers of paint and disgrace acquired throughout the day. What I intend to say is that you were the most beautiful creature I'd seen since the day I first laid eyes upon your mother. On the few nights I spent at home I would pass the hours just watching you and your mother sleeping ~she often kept you in our bed on the colder nights~ and I would think to myself how utterly amazing the two of you were…quite possibly the two most astonishing women in the entire world…and I would wonder at how it was that I came to be so unbelievably fortunate.

On my infinite list of regrets, I would have to include how I wish I'd been able to hold you more often than I did. But I could not. I trembled when I was sober and I would be afraid to hold you with such unstable hands, so I would drink to stop the trembling, but then, of course, I was drunk and consequently forbidden by Veda to touch you. It was torture that I could not hold you, truly nothing hurt me more than to see you in your mother's arms and know my embrace would be most unwelcome, but please believe me when I tell you I have held you a million times in my dreams since then…

London 1886

How empty a bustling city can look from the window of a desperate and lonely man's room. And how easy it would be to remedy such tragic isolation with something as simple as an embrace.

But for Vladimir it was not so easy. His pain could not be relieved by the touch of just anyone, and all those that could have healed him were gone. He cringed at the thought of some reeking whore smothering him with mounds of sweaty flesh and mock compassion, but that was his only remaining hope. Unless, of course, he could find the young and broken child he'd had before— the one that understood him, the one that did not try to devour him. He needed to find Mary.

≈

"I was beginnin' to wonder if you found another broker," Pinkney quipped as Vladimir took a seat next to him at the bar.

Vladimir said nothing and kept his head low. He had a less than honourable reputation, but to be seen associating with the likes of Lloyd Pinkney was something that even the lowest of men avoided whenever possible.

"Bring my friend *Mille'ovo* 'ere a drink on me!" Pinkney shot up from his stool and called out to the bartender loudly enough that the whole of the pub could hear. He made certain to say Vladimir's name as clearly as possible.

Vladimir grabbed Pinkney by the arm and forced him back into his seat. "I didn't come here to socialise with you."

"Oh," Pinkney feigned a look of disappointment. "And 'ere I thought you might 'ave missed me."

"I need to see Mary."

Pinkney looked momentarily puzzled. "Well *you* can't see 'er right now. She got prior engagements to attend to."

"Well then cancel them," Vladimir said with calmness and clarity.

Pinkney raised his brow, slightly shocked by the Russian's demand. "Why should I, after you been so rude to me?"

"I haven't even begun to be rude to you, Pinkney."

"I suppose thinkin' yourself too good to drink with me isn't rude," Pinkney teased.

"See here…I am not required to drink with you or socialise with you or skip through the streets hand-in-hand with you. You once called yourself a *business-man*, and so I am here to conduct a business transaction. I have the money and I want you to bring me the girl."

"I am more than 'appy to take your money an' bring you a girl, me friend…"

"Not just *any* girl. I need to see Mary."

It could have been the look of severity in Vladimir's eyes or the way his drawn face and neck tightened so unnaturally as he spoke her name, or possibly the absolute purity in his voice; not even Pinkney knew why it moved him so—only that it did. Something came from Vladimir that, for a single moment, found its way to Pinkney's tiny, rotting heart.

"All right then. I'll find *Mary* for you. But you're goin' to 'ave to pay twice the usual rate, for me trouble."

"Fine."

"An' you 'ave to do a favour for me, next time I might need one."

"Yes, fine." Vladimir hated to make that promise, but he would do whatever necessary to see the girl again.

"An' you 'ave to 'ave that drink with me now. Cheers, eh?"

Moscow 1869

Where there are pioneers, there must be sacrifices left in their wake, a willingness to stay on the path even if it means compromising the well-being of loved ones or oneself. And this was how the scientist and his muse drove each other to the brink of madness, experimenting nightly with Vladimir's concoctions. Sometimes the drugs would make them sick, sometimes euphoric. Sometimes they'd see stars and lizards and fairies, sometimes demons and hydra, or strange geometry and colours. Sometimes the drugs would do nothing remarkable at all. And sometimes all of the aforementioned conditions occurred at random intervals throughout one single evening.

When they slept, their dreams were warped and at times the pair were convinced that their dreams had been intertwined.

"Were you dreaming of strange cities? Because I was, and you were there and I am certain it was more than a mere crazed fancy," one would say.

"I dreamed this city also, and you were there. I clearly recall you wore—"

"A wig! A powdered wig like some sort of Parisian dandy!"

"Yes! My god! So it *was* you there…"

And so it would go each time; the men, amazed and bewildered by the experience, and becoming more and more deluded with each passing night.

Vladimir grew thinner and chalkier, more like a skeleton in time, while Ivo began to take on a swollen and waxy, yet emaciated appearance. Veda worried for her husband but refused to argue with him with baby Ana in the room. Vladimir's arguments were weak and nonsensical anyway, and Veda quickly realised how futile it was to spend what little time she had with the man fighting. So she tried to hold her tongue, but soon Vladimir was so short with her over every little thing that she bade him to go and spend all the time he desired with Ivo.

And I did leave, for the better part of each week, although I was losing all sense of time and its passage, so sometimes a day would feel to me as a week, and sometimes the other way around. When I would stay away for too long, Veda would come to Ivo's home to make sure we were still alive and to get money from Ivo. She never brought you with her and though this infuriated me at the time, looking back, I can scarcely blame her. She left you with your namesake on those visits, yet one more testament to what a good mother she was to you.

Sometimes on her visits I was lucid and would at first be glad to see her face, but then I could clearly decipher the stony look deep within her eyes as disappointment and pain. And sometimes she would make visits that I cannot even readily recall, though I think it would be accurate to believe that I was cruel to her each and every time. And Ivo was no better, sneering and wincing as though her struggle with the language pained him in some way, rolling his eyes as she spoke. We were lecherous toward her in our delirium; I can hazily remember making advances on her once in a while—thinking it not at all inappropriate as she was my wife—and forcing my reeking self upon her so immodestly in Ivo's doorway. I can still hear Ivo's voice as he called after her, "Oh, wonderful…you leave us now that he's worked himself into a frenzy! Now I should take care to fear for my manhood!" She said nothing, just turned away and walked on, but I was burning with a mix of desire and rage at his insinuation. And to imply it in front of Veda! I rushed upon him like a mad dog and came within an inch of hitting him in the mouth, and I knew it then…I knew I could not trust him fully. And over the weeks to follow, the chemicals would see to it that I trusted no one.

While time and chemistry will take their toll on truth, denial will ravage it beyond recognition. What Vladimir could not allow himself to recall about that night with Ivo was how he entertained the notion that he and Ivo could share something more intimate. It is true that he was angry with Ivo for making such a statement in front of Veda, and it is true that he lashed out at his friend as a result, but it is also true that later, after his anger and frustration subsided and a wave of euphoria washed back over his psyche, he approached Ivo with suggestions that he'd previously kept hidden deep inside.

"I cannot stop thinking about Veda," he said.

"Then perhaps you should go home and fuck her."

"That's not what I mean, Ivo. I cannot stop thinking about what you said to her."

"God, man! Are we going to go over that all night? You are going to absolutely *ruin* this wonderful feeling we've managed to create," he grinned. "We
may not have found exactly what we are looking for, but my, how much fun
it's been trying, eh?"

"Yes, we have been having a great deal of fun, haven't we?" Vladimir said
bashfully.

"Indeed. So let's not ruin it by talking about your wife."

"I love her, Ivo."

"Congratulations," he replied flatly.

"I love her, but she doesn't understand anything."

"Perhaps you should have married someone who speaks your language then."

Vladimir sighed heavily. "No, she doesn't understand *me*, or you…or this
project…this world…" he trailed off sadly.

Ivo nodded, lit a cigarette and stretched himself across a velvet couch.

"I…long to be close with someone who understands," Vladimir continued.
He was shaking to his bones. "I have desires…"

Ivo closed his eyes and let the smoke pour up and away from his mouth
like a dragon. "Would you like me to find us some women?"

"That's not what I meant…"

"We could pay a visit to your mother," Ivo laughed.

Vladimir narrowed his eyes. "Why are you so cruel to me? Why do you
make it so bloody difficult for me to say what I need to say?"

Ivo sat up and glared at Vladimir with remarkably sober eyes. "Because I
know what you are trying to say, and if you say it, I fear things will not be the
same between us."

Vladimir swallowed the massive lump in his throat. He wanted to say it
anyway, but he knew if he did he would lose Ivo forever.

"That's not who you are, Vladimir. You may be a broken man, perhaps even
an impotent man. You may even secretly loathe and fear women, but you are
not really a homosexual."

"How can you be so certain about it when I am not?"

"Vladimir, do you really, *truly* wish to be violated by me, the way we violate women? Do you *honestly* wish to be violated the way you've watched men do to those little whores you were raised with, or your *own* mother?"

"Please stop, Ivo…"

"I don't think you really want to fuck me or be fucked *by* me, Vladimir. I think what you really want to do is find some whore on the street, take her into an alley, strip her down, bend her over and break her into a million pieces and make her pay for the devastation that her sex has so coldly and painfully wrought upon you. Maybe it's what you want to do to all of those whores. Maybe it's what you secretly want to do to your own wife—"

"You are a vile man."

"She controls you, Vladimir. How do you expect your little daughter will grow up any different? She'll watch what her mother does to you, and she'll take heed. She'll manipulate and emasculate some poor flaccid wretch of her own, so one day you and your eunuch son-in-law can sit back and reminisce about how it used to be to have a cock—"

Ivo hit the floor with a great thump.

"Say one more thing, Kursk. Say *one more wretched thing* about my wife or child and I will beat you until you are unrecognisable."

Vladimir looked at his hand. There was a great gash across his knuckles where Ivo's teeth collided with vengeful flesh and bone.

Ivo chuckled callously, and pulled himself up from the floor. A bright ribbon of blood streaked his face and he said, "Well, I must have been mistaken. There's no rage within you, friend. No rage at all."

Vladimir paced the floor, cradling his bloodied hand, his mind racing and searching for a thread of clarity. As for Ivo, he'd still not been struck with enough force to suppress his malice.

"I find it very funny, " he said as he wiped the blood from his mouth, "that you'd lash out at me this way—to defend your wife's honour, when but a moment earlier you were ready to commit a most heinous act of adultery against her. Don't you find that ironic?"

He did. He found it ironic, he found it painful and he found it humiliating. And without another word he collected the devil in his head, stumbled out into the terrifying darkness, through the streets among the other devils disguised as vagrants and whores, and by twilight found his way home.

⟁

And that should have been the end. It should have been the last time I ever uttered his name or stepped foot in his home, but I was sick and desperate and fueled by passion and confusion and anger. We were quickly running out of money and Veda and I rarely spoke to each other, except to argue about where our next meal would come from. She had to sell most of her beautiful tapestries and one of her dresses and she did so without protest or tears. She said it was worth it to see you happily gobbling up your dinner each night, none the wiser to our troubles. She was so strong, Ana. I only once saw her break down, tears flowing down over her perfect jaw and onto that olive swan neck. When I asked her why she cried so, she said that now that she had to sell her good dress she feared that her flesh might be next. She said she cried because she had nothing else to pawn and she knew that if she sold her flesh she would never again have anything at all to give. I understood her then, I knew that her heart and soul would wither and die if she had to sell her body to keep her family alive. And I knew that I would be damned for all eternity for forcing her to such a fate.

So I went back to Ivo. But I did not grovel nor did I beg. This time I lied.

⟁

Ivo had no intention of letting him in, but Vladimir did not seem to notice or care. He pushed his way past the dishevelled young man, taking him by surprise and leaving him momentarily speechless.

"Before you say a word or attempt to throw me out, hear what I have to say…I think I've done it."

"Done what, exactly? You've been gone for weeks without your papers or materials so what could you have possibly done other than realize what a tremendous mistake you made in betraying me *yet again*?"

"Yes, but I had time…time to think about what was missing, and now I know. Now I…*we* can make this work. So we can stand here and argue like a married couple, or you can let the past lie and allow me to get to work."

And against his better judgement, that was just what Ivo did.

Vladimir toiled for hours, or pretended to toil for hours, at his table, swatting Ivo away every so often and convincing him that he was being a pest. But Ivo did not mind. There was something in the way that Vladimir had asserted himself, how he did not grovel at Ivo's feet, that left him fascinated and confused. Something had changed within Vladimir, Ivo was certain. He could see it in the way Vladimir carried himself and in the way his voice was steady and calm.

Late into the night the chemist worked. Just after the stroke of two, he called for Ivo to join him.

"Is this it?" Ivo asked softly, hopefully, as he stared at the glass tube of clear liquid.

"It is."

"Well, let's get to it!" Ivo laughed.

Vladimir smiled and handed him the vial.

"Where's yours?"

"I rationed mine out already," he held up a small glass of something that looked just the same.

"Oh my god. This is it. This is *really* it, isn't it? I'm proud of you Vladimir. I'm proud of *us*."

There was the faint tinkling of the glasses as the men tapped them together. Ivo swallowed his without fear or hesitation. He trusted his partner, or at least trusted himself to be the more callous and conniving of the two. Vladimir drank his down smoothly a second later.

"*God* that tasted bitter! Such an odd under taste."

"Funny, mine tasted almost exactly like vodka," said Vladimir.

Within the hour, Ivo was nearly unconscious. They had talked for a while, mostly nonsense, although Ivo remained lucid enough to remark that he felt very tired and confused. Perhaps the measurements would need to be adjusted a bit. Vladimir agreed. He would look into it.

"I had the strangest dream last night," Vladimir began. His voice was purposefully soft and hypnotic. "I dreamed that Veda was one of my father's girls."

"A...whore..." Ivo slurred.

"Yes, Ivo. She was a whore."

"Like your...mother..." Ivo smiled wearily, wanting very much to laugh at his own joke, but having no recollection of how one, exactly, goes about laughing.

"Indeed. Just like my mother." It saddened, but did not surprise Vladimir that Ivo could be so caustic even when drugged. "Anyway, Veda was a whore, and I came to the house as a client, but upon my arrival there were only three girls there for me to choose from."

"Veda...an' your mother...eh?"

"Yes, one was Veda, and one was my mother...but the third...the third was just a child. She was so beautiful, but barely even a woman."

"Well...did you...fuck 'er?" The words spilled from Ivo's mouth, carelessly and without grace.

"No, you bastard. She was my daughter."

"That's disgusting," Ivo snarled like a sick animal, then grinned. "You can pass 'er on to me then...if you don' want 'er." Again, he tried to laugh, but his heavy head just swayed on his neck like a rag doll.

"No, I'd sooner murder her than see her with a man like you," Vladimir said calmly. "That's why I've done what I've done."

Still Ivo smiled until his jaw became like lead and he could not hold it closed.

"You'll be asleep soon. Very deeply, and for a very long time, and when you eventually wake up, I will be gone. I will have taken my family and these papers and whatever money you have in this house and I will be so far away from you and this city that it may take you the rest of your life to find me, if you ever do. And if you *do* find me, I will simply kill you where you stand. But none of this will matter in a few moments. You'll be sound asleep, and I will be a ghost."

It was so easy, Ana, so easy in fact, I chided myself over and over again for not thinking of it sooner. Then again, there was a great degree of trust to be fostered between Ivo and myself, and without it, my plan would have certainly failed. And if I am to be truthful, many things in my head had changed and shifted during the months we spent experimenting. There were thoughts introduced to me in my sleep that I never could have imagined in my waking hours, and I could see things in a way I had not before. It sounds fantastic, I know, but I tell you something within my brain was altered by my strange chemistry, and I nearly felt regret that I would be unable to carry on with Ivo and his plan. I half-think it could have worked...or at least come very, very close.

It was a long and uncomfortable journey toward the unknown future of the Millerovo family. For the first time Vladimir felt fortunate to have so little, as there was less to worry with on their travels, and the baby was handful enough. Veda did not mind this; she was elated to be leaving Moscow, and soon grew even happier once Vladimir announced that they would be returning to her home in

Constanta to collect themselves and figure out a plan. They would be safe from Kursk there, surrounded by Veda's protective father and brothers, and it would be nice for Veda's parents to meet their granddaughter. Vladimir scoured his memory: had he ever told Kursk where he went on holiday? He knew he'd said Romania, but had he named the town? Maybe it wouldn't matter; after all, Ivo had taken enough drugs to erase substantial details from his mind.

Veda was staring at her husband. The barren landscape flowed past the window of the train like a wild river, and she remembered the first time she rode on the train with him. The car they rode in now was nicer, but the odours were the same, a pungent mix of the residue of human bodies and spices. And Vladimir, well, he was a shell of a man then as he was now. She winced at his strained face and pale, trembling hands.

"What troubles you, my love?"

He broke free from his obsessive wondering and looked at his wife, their beautiful sleeping child in her arms.

"I was just thinking"

"About *him*?"

Vladimir glanced away, guiltily.

"We will be safe with my family."

"For a while, yes."

"Perhaps. Or perhaps we would be safe there forever?" she asked hopefully.

"Let's not get ahead of ourselves. We shall see." He patted her on the knee. "Let's just get to Constanta, then we shall see, yes?"

Veda leaned in and kissed her husband softly on the jaw. He smiled at her and closed his eyes, praying for a bit of slumber to release him from his fear.

⤜⤛

"Dimi? Wake up, Dimi."

Vladimir flinched and rubbed his eyes vigorously until the blur before him transformed into a real creature, a beautiful creature he once called Katya. She looked as he remembered her, perhaps a bit older, a bit more tattered. The gruesome mark she wore at her neck was new. And that she made no reflection in the black window of the train car was presumably new as well. The Katya he knew was in love with her own reflection and he couldn't imagine she'd ever shed it by choice.

It was quite a strange scene there on the train. Veda and Ana to his right, and his dead first love sitting so casually across from him. This did not alarm Vladimir. He could see no good sense in being afraid. It was very likely a hallucination or a dream, and even if it wasn't, what would be accomplished by causing a commotion, other than to startle his wife and wake the baby?

"Why are you here?"

The spectre ignored his question. *"Is this your wife?"* she cooed, gazing dreamily at Veda, who was sound asleep. *"She's lovely, Dimi. You did very well."*

"Yes, well…I've hardly been waiting for your approval," he whispered harshly. "Now state your purpose."

"I do hope you serve her well," she smiled coyly. *"She is a fiery thing. A creature of passion and light—"*

"*Stop*. Stop looking at her, *demon*!" he hissed. You will look only at *me*, not my wife or my daughter."

But still, the ghost stared at Veda with black, glassy eyes. Her mouth was opened slightly, seductively, although no breath escaped. *"You have a child? I cannot see her. I cannot see anything that has yet to have a fire lit within its body. The younger the child, the fainter the spark."* Now her eyes drifted back to Vladimir. *"But in your wife, it is a raging fire. Tell me Dimi, do you fan the flames or do you pray for merciful rain to come and extinguish her for you?"*

"Did you come back from the dead just to say lustful things to me? Did you not have enough of it when we were children?"

"I came with a message from your friend Ivo. He never woke up, you know. His heart stopped only an hour after you left his home. Only one hour—after

you poisoned him and stole his money. He asked me to come to you and tell you that as soon as he is strong enough, as soon as he has been here long enough to understand the laws that apply on this side, he will find you and he will make you suffer."

Vladimir felt his heart sink and his blood go hot. He broke a hard sweat and his eyes filled with tears. "Ivo died?"

"Yes, and I tell you this as a friend—do not count on having too many days of peace. Time works differently here, and it won't be long before he learns how to haunt you. Sleep well tonight, Dimi. It could be the last restful night you have."

"How do I know I'm not dreaming you?"

"Do you dream of me often?"

"Only in night terrors."

She smiled, though her eyes spoke of something sadder. *"I miss you, Dimi. You were good to me and I squandered it. But I learned my lesson. I learned that men can be brutal, so if you find one that adores you, it's best to hold on to him."*

"It would seem you learned it too late."

"Perhaps, but at least I learned. Some people never do—even in death."

Vladimir closed his eyes, feeling quite sick to his stomach. The air in the car was colder now, but it did not ease his fever.

"What will you have learned, when it's your turn, Dimi? Come and tell me, won't you?"

Vladimir opened his eyes and she was gone. He did not sleep again that night, and he watched the sun flood the horizon with burning eyes.

Veda was bursting with excitement as the carriage neared Constanta. The landscape was just as she'd remembered it: golden fields and chalky hills, blue sky over blue water. And it was warm. She'd forgotten what it was to be warm.

Vladimir was overcome by the smell of the salty sea. Salt was for purification. Salt could cleanse him; it could erode his past, his crimes, his humiliation.

Beneath it he could bury all of it; he could even bury Ivo. He suddenly could not help but to think of the holiday spent there. He wanted to taste rum on his lips again. He wanted to taste Veda.

He shifted tightly in his seat, uncertain of what to do with such a foreign sensation as sober arousal. At that moment, Veda looked up from the child in her arms and smiled.

"It is this place, I tell you. It stirs things inside of you."

"Things that wish only to hibernate in Moscow," Vladimir replied and smiled.

Veda laughed out loud and Vladimir could not resist joining her. This prompted Ana to giggle softly at first, then shriek wildly at her parents' laughter.

Vladimir dove across the carriage to Veda's bench, gently so as not to crush Ana, but with enough force that it took Veda by surprise. Cradling her head in his hands, he kissed her deeply, in a way that he seldom did anymore. When it became apparent that he could not stop himself, Veda whispered in between heated breaths that he should stop because of the baby.

"She's young enough still, she's fine..." he growled and ran his tongue along his wife's beautiful neck.

"And what of the coachman? He'll toss us out on the road if we do not mind ourselves!"

She laughed as her husband found his way beneath her skirts and began to tickle her thigh.

"Vladimir! *Really!*"

He let go and playfully slumped down onto the bench in defeat. "As you wish, my love. I will humbly remain your obedient and frustrated servant."

"Hush. There will be plenty of time for you to serve me later," she smiled. "Look! We are almost there!"

Vladimir turned his eyes to the window and saw the marketplace where he'd first met Veda's father. They would soon be at her home, and this was fine by Vladimir. At that moment in time, he did not care about Ivo, or ghosts, or drink, or the experiment.

As he looked from the window to his young wife's face, her happiness suddenly became the only important thing in the world.

"*Mama!*" Veda cried out before Vladimir even stepped out of the carriage.

Lavinia came running across the hilly, orchard-lined terrain. The two women embraced, and Lavinia wasted no time taking Ana in her arms. They spoke so feverishly in their own tongue that Vladimir could barely understand. Soon, Veda's grandmother Iona, who had taken a little bit longer to make her way from the house, joined them. The women were so taken with Veda and the newest female to join the Sera clan that they scarcely noticed Vladimir hovering behind.

Vladimir cleared his throat. "I suppose I shall just wait over here with the dogs."

Lavinia clasped her hands to her mouth and came towards the tall man. "Oh, Vladimir! Look at you!" She wrapped her arms around her son-in-law and squeezed tightly. "You are sick, yes? You look tired. I will feed you!" She spun around. "Luca! Come help your brother with their belongings!"

Vladimir and Veda both turned to see Luca slowly emerging from the house. He looked just the same, a beautiful replica of his sister, only darker now than she. He hesitated, then went to Veda and greeted her with a kiss that was strange enough to give Vladimir pause. It was not that he kissed her on the mouth, but the passion that seemed to incite it that disturbed him. Even Lavinia and Iona stared with strange expressions, but the moment was fleeting and before he could speak of it, Luca approached Vladimir and kissed him quickly on each cheek.

"You were right to bring her back to us, but I still see you as you are," Luca whispered.

"Good! Now help your brother carry that chest," Lavinia called out again.

The men hoisted the heavy trunk into the air and as they did Luca caught his eyes with a piercing look and said quietly so his mother could not hear, "You and I are not brothers."

Vladimir looked straight ahead and simply said, "I know."

As they neared the door, Iona, speaking to Vladimir for the first time since their arrival, told the men to leave the trunk outside and fetch the other bags.

As they began to walk back up the hill, she called for Vladimir to come back. He did so, and she pulled him gently away.

"It's good to see you again, Iona," Vladimir said with an awkward politeness.

She smiled dryly. "Same to you, travelling man."

Vladimir thought it to be an odd thing to call him, but did not question the old woman.

"I…should help Luca…"

She nodded. "You may bring your possessions into our home, but you leave those ghosts outside when you come in, yes?"

Vladimir swallowed hard. "Ghosts?"

Iona nodded again, slowly. "The ones you brought with you. They are not welcome here." She patted him lightly on the cheek, smiled again, and walked away.

❦

There was plenty of room now in the Sera home. Since Veda's departure, Gregor and Alexi had both married and built houses of their own nearby. Luca spent little time at home and, although he was not betrothed to any particular young woman, he was cultivating a reputation in town as a scoundrel. He was known to have been with a different girl five out of seven nights in a row, so the town gossips said. It was also said that his girls were getting younger and younger, as the twenty-two-year-old was running through the girls his own age much too quickly. This did not please Lavinia and Alexandru, but they had faith that their son would grow out of this behaviour in time.

That night, the feast was a large one. Alexandru and Lavinia, Iona, Luca, Veda, Vladimir, baby Ana, Gregor and his wife Silvia, and Alexi, his wife, Elina and their two-year-old son Andrei came together for the first time to celebrate their ever-growing family. It was a good celebration, too, the tension between Vladimir and Luca stifled by the sounds of laughter and cheer.

When the wine was passed, Vladimir politely refused but Alexandru insisted and Veda gave him a subtle permissive nod, so he drank…but with some reserve.

Afterward, as the table began to look more and more like a storm had washed over it, Luca excused himself, despite Lavinia's protest.

It could have been the wine, but Vladimir could not resist the chance to get back at Luca for his earlier remark, so he spoke up.

"Lavinia, Luca is a young man with a wild heart. He needs to have his freedom. How else will he ever find his heart's desire, the way I have?" Then he looked to Veda and kissed her on the cheek. A round of suggestive laughter rose from the table. "And if I may be so bold, I say let him go on!" He smiled wickedly at Luca. "There is time still for us to catch up."

Luca glared at his brother-in-law, but could say nothing. Under any other circumstance he would have beaten the man for such demeaning words, but all he could do was take a deep breath and kiss his mother on the cheek before walking out the door.

The women cleared the table as the men wandered outside to take in the warm night air. Silvia took Ana and Andrei and played with them as the other women worked.

"She wants children of her own so badly," Lavinia whispered to Veda, "but they are having trouble getting her with child."

"Is because Gregor does not believe in prayer," Iona chimed in.

"Hush, Mama," Lavinia scolded. "That is not the reason, and don't let Silvia hear you say such things!"

Iona shrugged and continued to clear away the scraps.

Veda turned to Silvia. "Would you and Gregor like to take Ana this evening?"

Silvia's round face lit up. She was a very pretty young woman. "Oh, yes! That would be wonderful!"

"She's a good child. She won't give you any trouble."

Elina joined in. "I'm sure you and that tall husband of yours would like to have some time alone! Thank God that our families all live so close. It never seems to be any trouble to have Andrei stay with his grandparents now and then, is it?"

Lavinia smiled. "None at all." She turned to Veda. " And when Ana comes back tomorrow, I shall take her and you can take Vladimir into town if you like."

With that settled, Veda found her husband and took him by the hand. When they were away from her father and brothers she said, "We have the evening alone, and tomorrow if we want it."

"Really?"

She nodded.

"Gentlemen!" Vladimir called out gleefully, "I bid you goodnight! My wife and I are suddenly going for a stroll."

"Thank you, Gregor!" Veda shouted over her shoulder, then laughed, knowing that her brother would be puzzled by it until he went inside to see his wife with a tiny and unexpected houseguest.

❧

"Is this the place?"

Veda said yes. She felt her way in the darkness over the rocks, following the sounds of the water and guiding Vladimir until they reached a suitable place to rest.

"This is where I met you that night," she said. "It is one of my favourite places. Tomorrow I will show you some others."

"I would like that very much." Vladimir reached for his wife and kissed her.

Soon, he was undressing her, and even though it was too dark to see her, he could feel her beauty. He took his time kissing her entire body, tasting her skin like he never had before, and for a second he felt ashamed that he hadn't learned to enjoy her this way sooner. He wasn't drunk now, and that was good. This was what it was supposed to be like. She pawed at him and ground herself against his thigh and said breathlessly that she wanted to be like animals, here on the shore of her beloved sea, exposed to the sky.

When it was done, Veda was exhausted and had no trouble at all falling asleep on the rocks. Vladimir, also exhausted, did not find sleep so easily. His mind began to trick him, thinking he heard voices or saw people standing where no man could venture. At first it was just sounds, possibly his name that he heard rising from the water as it slapped against the stones, but as the dawn grew near, he could hear the words clearly:

"Murderer. Animal. Coward. Addict. Failure…"

He face tightened. "Very clever, how the mind is. You are just water. You are not real."

But then words became sentences, purposeful and specific:

"Do you see how it works in tandem for you, friend? Do you see how you cannot truly be a man until you've destroyed? Sex and death, sex and desecration…they are your only companions, and they will consume you…I promise you this. You will consume your wife and your daughter as your vices will consume you…"

"Veda, are you awake? I want to go…" he whispered to his sleeping wife, but she did not respond.

"If it weren't for the fact that it was all at my expense, I'd almost be proud of you the way you so callously left me for dead, stole from me, and now have so little capacity for guilt that you should spend the night fucking your bitch in heat. And my, how like a bitch she was, on all fours! Bravo, friend…it's a remarkable thing, really. Did you know it was days before anyone found me? Did you know I felt it when my heart seized?"

"Veda?" He touched her face and she turned toward him, only it was the pale, battered face of Katya that he saw, loosely pivoting on a twisted and scarred neck.

Vladimir jumped and pulled his hand away in terror.

"It wasn't my idea, Dimi," she said sympathetically. *"He's just toying with your mind."*

He blinked and saw Veda again, stirring just a bit, but peaceful none the less. He choked back his tears and tried to regain his breath. Everything was the same, the air, the sea, his wife…everything but himself, and there was really nothing else to do, so he covered his face with his hands and remained that way until morning.

When Veda awoke and saw her husband in such a state, she was afraid. For all of the trouble and strife they'd been through in Moscow, she'd never seen him so terrified and broken.

And when she touched him he flinched, as those who have been so brutally violated are wont to do, and he said, "Veda, please help me. I need to be cleansed."

Iona sat before him in the sun-drenched room, gazing calmly at her grandson-in-law. Veda and Lavinia had taken Ana and gone to the market, Alexandru was on the boat, and Luca had yet to return from his nightly carousing.

Vladimir was not so calm. He was weary and quiet, but not at all calm. He thought he might burst if Iona did not speak soon.

But she did not speak, not for a very long time, and Vladimir did not burst. He trembled, and his stomach turned again and again, forcing small amounts of acidic fluid into his mouth, which burned him just as badly on the way back down, but still he did not explode.

At last, the old woman uttered a sentence, though it was not what he'd hoped to hear.

"I am quiet for so long because I do not know how to solve this riddle. How does one cleanse the devil?" she said.

"Why do you say I am a devil? You've said it from the first moment you met me, and still you say it now."

She smiled and her tightly drawn mouth became a series of tiny dry rivers. "Well, perhaps you are not the devil, himself, but is there any true difference between the devil and his instruments?"

"Is that what you think I am? An instrument?"

"Yes. *You* are the instrument and *your actions* are the songs of selfishness that the devil plays. When you serve yourself, you are serving him. So you see, one in the same."

"Then I need to be a more selfless man."

"It is too late. Everything is moving now and there is no undoing what has been done…and we both know what has been done. A man does not travel with vengeful spirits for no reason, eh?"

"There is no solid evidence of such a thing, do you know that? I've neither heard nor seen anything concrete to support the idea that I…I did what I keep dreaming about, or imagining, or whatever it is that's happening," he stammered. "I could be going mad! It could be something I ate or drank… anything at all!"

Iona nodded. "It could be," she said. "But it is not. And you know this. It is why you come to me. Face yourself, Vladimir."

He thought he might cry. "I…I cannot…" he closed his eyes and exhaled loudly. "I did not intend to— "

"Do not say it aloud to me! I am not your confessor, as I am not willing to be a witness to your atrocities," the old woman hissed. Then she said quietly, "And if you tell me, and I am asked, I will have to say what I know. But if you never said it to me, then I know nothing, *da*?"

He understood. "Then there is nothing at all I can do? I am damned? Is that what I am to accept?"

"No, no…you will always have choices. You cannot go back, but you will find yourself at the crossroads again. You will have a choice. And so will my granddaughter. You always have. And though you cannot make it better, you can keep it from getting worse."

Vladimir lowered his head. It wasn't the worst news he could have received, but it certainly wasn't the best. He wanted a miracle; he wanted a talisman, or something magic to relieve him from his conscience. It didn't matter that he didn't believe in these things, he knew they were the only things that could save him now. He thanked Iona for her counsel and made his way to the door.

"I'd say you are a good boy, Vladimir Millerovo, but you are not," Iona called after him. "But still, you are worthy of this knowledge. "

"What's that?"

"The angels play instruments, too."

I must have appeared no less broken when I saw your mother after my talk with Iona, because she decided it was necessary for us to go to the baths. They were healing, she said, and could wash away my ills, and I was willing to try anything to leave the ghosts of Moscow behind.

It would take them several hours by carriage to travel the dusty road to the Mangalia. Vladimir was solemn the whole way and this worried Veda even more.

Things had been so good just the previous day, but since then, something inside of Vladimir had shifted, causing a great rift between them once again.

"Whatever it is, my love, the baths will heal," she offered. "No matter how terrible."

He tried to smile at her, but fell short.

"Is it *that* terrible?"

The colour drained from his face and his eyes became like polished glass, but he said nothing, and she knew it was, indeed, *that* terrible.

⤛

There are few moments in my life that I can recall with such vivid detail that it should engage all of my senses, but the day I spent at Mangalia shall stay with me for the remainder of my life. When I think of it, I do not smell the rank stench of the river outside this cold, grim flat or human waste, but the salts and oddly comforting metals that rose from the springs. I do not hear the wretched cries of hungry children or the sound of men slaving away at the ports, or the cackle of gossiping women and greedy street vendors, but the echo of water in the natural coves and chambers. I hear Veda's deep calm voice telling me that I will be fine; I hear her whispering something so softly in her own language over and over again ~ a mantra, a protection, something for me because she loves me. I do not taste bile and vitriol on my tongue, but the salt of the earth and the memory of Veda. I see her before me, her dark skin glowing above the surface of the blue water and muted below, and I feel her pouring that water over my head and onto my chest as though it were my baptism. I am not cold; I am not alone in this place. I am warm and I am loved and I will continue to be until I open my eyes.

⤛

The ghosts did not haunt Vladimir while he was at Mangalia. Legend would say that they could not, due to the intricate chemistry of the place; the saline and iodine, among many other elements, served as a barrier of sorts, absorbing all matter that sought to harm its pilgrims. There was no true scientific reason for this, but no one seeking refuge there ever seemed to mind. It was a place of faith, this holy bath, and he did not ever want to leave.

Vladimir contemplated telling his wife what he'd done. As far as she knew, Vladimir went to Ivan that day to settle things once and for all. He was owed money for his work, and he and Ivan had a falling out about it. There was an argument, and when Ivan went to collect himself, Vladimir took his papers and money and fled. It was presumed that Ivan did not immediately notice this, as he did not come calling while the family packed their few belongings and quietly made their way out of town. Veda could not understand why her husband was so nervous about the whole thing; after all, he only took what he was due. Vladimir explained that due to all of the experimentation, Ivan was not in his right mind and would indeed be angry with him for his actions. He was no longer the rational person Vladimir once admired, which was a true statement, even with the recent turn of events. He wanted so badly to tell her the true story, to release the burning pressure from his heart, but he could not find the words. He could not make this heavy confession to his wife. So she would stay at his side, trying to heal this mysterious ailment, worrying and speculating what her beloved's tremendous secret was, while he remained quiet and tried to pretend that ravenous guilt was not eating him alive.

The days to come were not easy for Vladimir. His wife remained troubled, which in turn made Ana fussier than usual; and it was most difficult for him to face Iona. She had few words for him, cruel or kind, but the look in her eyes was enough to drive a man to drink. But the real tension came from any and all dealings with Luca. The intuitive young man resisted no chance to jab at his brother-in-law's open wounds.

Vladimir tried to avoid him for the better part of each day, and Luca seldom came home at night, but it was only a matter of time before their paths would cross.

"You've really accomplished something, blinding my sister the way you have."

"I'm sure I don't know what you're talking about, Luca."

"There was a time she would have seen what sort of man you are, the way I do and the way my grandmother does. But she loves you far deeper than you are worth, and she is blinded by it. I don't think you have any understanding of what you've done."

Vladimir fixed his gaze upon the young man. "I am trying now to make amends. I know I should have never taken her to Moscow. I should have never gone back at all. But at the time, I knew nothing else. So, now, I am here and I will do my best to make her happy."

"You never should have taken her anywhere."

"There was nothing for me here…no work…"

"No! *You* never should have taken *her*—"

"Taken her where? Away from you? Is that what you mean?"

Luca burned and seethed with hatred for his brother-in-law, but Vladimir did not relent.

"I see how you watch her, how you leer at her like a beast. I saw how you kissed her when we arrived. She is your *sister*…your *blood*. You are so quick to condemn me for my ills, but what sickness lies within your heart, Luca, that allows you to lust for your own flesh and blood?"

As the words spilled from his mouth Vladimir felt sickened by his bitter hypocrisy. He saw his own mother in his arms again and remembered how he longed to tear her apart, and for a terrible moment, Luca looked deeply into him and saw it too.

"I know exactly what you are, Millerovo. And soon enough, Veda will know it too."

"Then I wish you'd tell me, because I do not know."

But Luca was already gone.

By early winter, Vladimir had taken all he could of Luca's daily threats and insinuations, true though they may have been. Veda might have been content

121

to remain with her family for the rest of her life, but was not too blinded by her own comfort to see how worn her husband was becoming. He had plenty of demons of his own, and did not need one more in Luca. And though it broke her heart, when Vladimir announced that it was time for the Millerovo family to move on, Veda did not protest.

And move on they did, not stopping until they reached northern Africa in 1872, at which point Veda threatened to turn around and go back to Constanta—child in tow—if Vladimir did not agree to let them settle down temporarily.

Ana had been like a ghost throughout that journey. What should have been a time of discovery and learning for the child was mired in confusion and chaos, though her mother and father scarcely spoke for those many weeks. But there were noisy trains, and noisier people; sometimes just *so many people*, speaking so many different languages all at once. There were so many smells, most of them terrible. Animals, bodies—all of it was too much. The child sought constant refuge in the arms of her distracted parents, burying her face in her mother's bosom, or in the rough jacket her father often wore, but their smells were not as she remembered. They did not smell like themselves. She did not have the words then, but if she could have, she would have identified the scents of exhaustion and fear.

And then there was the light. It changed so much as they traveled, growing brighter and brighter with each day, showing the dust that had begun to choke them all. This painful, harsh light reflecting on yellow sand. Everything was filthy, all the time. Everything was dry, and all the things that were once beautiful were either dying, or crumbling into nothing. She did not see anything green again until Algeria.

Ana was young enough that she should not have remembered these things, but she did. She could not forget them no matter how hard she tried.

⤚

In my delirium, I nearly agreed to let the two of you go back. I could have kept going and simply disappeared, and as it turns out, that would have been the very best thing I could have done for you both. But as I realised what I was about to lose, I surrendered to your mother's wishes and we found a little house to rent that very day. That was in Algiers, though I'm not certain you'd remember it, and it's probably for the best that you don't. I was very sick then, in a different manner than what you'd witness in later years, but in a terrible state just the same. In Romania I'd believed myself to be haunted, but the more I pondered this, the more I saw what nonsense it was. I did not believe in ghosts. My troubles were the machinations of my own damned conscience, nothing more. And for a while, I believed this. But everywhere we went, he was there, taunting me. Sometimes I could hear his voice in a crowd, other times I would see him just as I'd turn the corner. As far as I was concerned, Ivan Kursk was alive and well and going to great lengths to find and take his revenge upon me for my betrayal.

Vladimir was beyond understanding the cues that would have suggested his encounters with Kursk to be imaginary. His mind was fragile and he did not think it odd that Ivo not only knew where he was at all times, but would know what Vladimir was thinking. He did not yet accept that his dealings with Ivo were shrouded in the same unsettling haze that was present in his dreams. And then there were the hallucinations. Katya still visited every now and then, but Vladimir dismissed it as a result of the stress put upon him by Ivo's presence. The thread between the real and imagined was pulled taut and would soon begin to unravel completely.

Veda implored him to find work. Perhaps it would ease his conscience a bit if they were not living solely on the "stolen money". Vladimir agreed, but quickly learned that there was little work for a stranger within the city. He would tell Veda that he'd found work on the docks, and that yes, it was beneath him, but it was better than nothing, when really he'd only managed to find some rather unsavoury Frenchmen who would convince him that his days were better spent drinking and gambling. They were long and hard, the hours he put in, but that was a sacrifice Vladimir was happy to make for his family.

London 1887

Vladimir waited another full day before there was a knock at the door. Thank god, he thought. Pinkney came through for him. He's found Mary.

But the girl standing in the hall was not Mary. She was young and had dark hair, but it was not Mary.

"Who are you?"

"Who do you want me to be?"

He was always struck by the willingness of these girls to shed their identities without hesitation. At times it could make it difficult for him to enjoy them.

"Where's Mary?"

"I can be Mary," she cooed.

"No. No, you can't."

She smiled awkwardly and fidgeted in the doorway, waiting for further instruction.

"You may as well go," Vladimir said. He wasn't angry. Not at her.

"Or I could stay and take care of you," she offered.

Vladimir shook his head and sighed. "No. It's no good. I needed Mary. I'm sorry I've wasted your time."

"Who's this Mary? Is she one of Mister Pinkney's? 'Cause I never heard of 'er."

"I don't know. She's just a girl."

"And wot do ya think I am, a bloody wolfhound?"

"Of course not. But you're not Mary."

"Right then. I'm gonna leave now, 'cause if I have to hear the name Mary come outta yer mouth one more time, I just might scream. Cheers!"

⮑

Vladimir sat alone in the corner of the pub, drinking and waiting for Pinkney to slither in, which he did, moments later. Pinkney made a beeline for his client.

"So now you're sending me girls away, Mille'ovo? I s'pose you find 'em beneath you," he grinned.

"I asked for Mary, and you sent someone that was distinctly *not* Mary."

"You know, most of my customers can't even tell 'em apart. But not you! You know 'em by name. Impressive."

"Let's not draw this out Pinkney. I want Mary."

"Bloody 'ell! I don' even know any Mary!"

"Then why did you say you did before?" Vladimir slammed his glass on the table. "Why did you promise me you'd find her?"

"You was in a rage, near as I could tell! I just said what I had to, to shut you up!"

Vladimir considered bashing his glass into Pinkney's face, then thought better of it. The pub had fallen silent in anticipation, being full of patrons who might have paid to see Pinkney beaten to a pulp, but Vladimir did not sate their bloodlust.

"Just find her," he said calmly. "Find the dark-haired girl you sent me before."

Pinkney's rodent eyes welled up with frustration. He stared at Vladimir, feeling a bit sorry for him, unsure of what to do.

"Mate…truly, I don' know what to tell you. If I knew this Mary, I'd get 'er for you. But I don'. Look, I know I give you trouble, but I don' *mean* it. I grown quite fond a' you after all this time, so curse me bloody soul if I'm lyin', but I don' know who she is."

Vladimir cast his eyes to the ceiling. He didn't want to believe, but he knew in his bones that Pinkney was telling the truth, so he dismissed the man without another harsh word.

Algiers 1872

Algiers was not the sanctuary the Millerovo family had hoped. Vladimir was gone for hours, sometimes days on end, and Veda did not feel safe in the city, especially not with Ana at her hip. Algiers was beautiful enough, not so different from what Veda's Constanta would eventually become, but she was dangerous, filled with strangers and the infinite dark possibilities that come with the unknown.

Such possibilities assaulted Veda one balmy afternoon in the market place, upon discovering that Ana had wandered into the crowd while Veda purchased their dinner. She tore through the sea of consumers, shrieking her child's name and grasping at every small child she saw, tearfully hoping the next would be hers. She was suffocating under her fear, the world around her having fallen into a thick haze, like syrup, time creeping along painfully, putting centuries between her and her daughter.

A soft, dark hand fell upon her shoulder and she heard someone saying the words '*Madame, Madame*'.

Veda turned to see a heavy, dark-skinned woman holding the hand of a small girl. *Her* girl. Veda fell to her knees and sobbed, gathering up and embracing her child with something close to violence.

"Thank you," Veda said, "oh, *merci, Madame!*" It was nearly all the French she knew.

The woman responded with words Veda could not understand. She looked at her daughter, and then she looked at the crowd. She was a stranger here. The bright sun did not comfort her, nor did the colourful tents or breezy palms. She was alone with her child, unable to communicate, and unable to contain her tears.

The black woman placed her arm around Veda and whispered something that sounded sympathetic.

"I wish I could understand you," Veda cried. She gripped Ana's tiny hand with unnecessary pressure, determined not to lose the girl again. She felt sick, and embarrassed, like a child herself. "I know you do not understand me either, but thank you...*merci*. I just want to go home now."

When Vladimir returned, Ana was asleep, and though Veda seemed to rest quietly on the bed, she was awake and distraught. Vladimir fell onto the bed, reeking of liquor and sweat. He reached clumsily for her, groping at her breasts, and kissing her back with a sticky mouth.

Veda pulled away, disgusted. "I nearly lost our daughter today while you were out...*working*."

"*Working*? What is that in your voice I hear? Are you implying that I may have been doing something else?"

"I do not care what you do anymore. Did you even hear what I said, or were you too busy weaving your own defence? I almost lost our child in the crowd and I could not ask for help, because I cannot speak the way people do here!"

"Veda, the only place you have ever felt happy was in Constanta. What should we do then? Go back where I am hated? Or where we could be found?"

"No. I suppose your selfish deeds have left us with our hands tied."

Vladimir struck her, open-handed, across her mouth and then there was silence.

"Veda..."

She was still. She did not speak or cry or curse him. She licked her lip, checking for blood.

"Veda, please—I don't..."

And Veda said nothing. She sat up in the bed, the white blanket pooled around her torso, her olive skin reflecting a ray of moonlight like the sea.

"Veda," Vladimir bowed his head and rested it at her breast, "this is not me. I have never…I would *never…*"

"But you did. *You just did.*"

"It's not me, love. I was drinking. I know I broke my promise, but I've been in so much pain…"

"I know you've been drinking. You've been drinking since we came here. Do you think I am a fool?"

He shook his head. "I'm sorry."

Veda stared into nothingness. In the quiet room she could hear the soft breathing of their precious daughter, dreaming and unaware of the ugliness that had crept in through the dark.

Vladimir carried on. He was sick, he said. Haunted still, as he'd been in Constanta.

"The only thing haunting you, Vladimir, is your conscience."

"I do not disagree, but the nature of the ghost doesn't matter, only that it is relentless in its desire to destroy me."

"So you'd let it destroy us, too?" Veda touched her lip. The swelling had begun.

"Never."

"That is good to hear," she finally turned to face him, "because if you ever lay a hand on me again, I will cut out your poisoned heart and feed it to the wild dogs that run our street at night."

"If I ever lay a hand on you again, I will personally give you the knife."

⌘

And I meant it, too. I truly did. And though it is a terrible thing to say, I almost kept that promise, at least in letter, if not in spirit.

I tried to stay sober, as well, but it was a difficult thing to do in the company I kept. They were a strange group, these men, these pirates, really. They'd come from Tunis and Rabat, although two of the men were Dutch, and though they fancied themselves to be descended from greatness, there was no reason to believe them anything more than drunken, unemployed sailors, but their talk was convincing and the game was fun, so I played along. If I am to purge my filthy soul to you then I cannot omit my dealings with 'the pirates.' Usually we drank and schemed. And on a few occasions, we even committed petty crimes ~ thievery, mostly, of local vendors and businesses along the harbour. And once, in a drunken stupor, we commandeered a tiny fishing boat, and left it beached some miles down the shore. I was fine with this, as awful as it was, but of course, it was only a matter of time before too much drink and even more bravado found us in a most heinous situation and I had to sever ties with my mates. I was not a witness to the entire event, but I know a young woman was hurt, for I had listened to her muffled screams from behind a fisherman's shack. I listened to those screams and I did nothing. I knew then it was time to leave Algiers. I didn't need any more ghosts haunting me.

We found passage on a cargo ship bound for the West Indies within the week. It was hardly suitable for a woman and child, but then again, neither was Algiers.

London 1887

London at night never seemed warm. The season didn't matter, or perhaps it just didn't matter to Vladimir. He was always cold, his skin always felt damp, which was why he rarely went out. Or so he convinced himself.

There were plenty of girls on the streets, lingering in the shadows like the kin of rats, but these creatures ran towards men rather than away from them. Vladimir paid no attention to the light-haired girls, and only paused momentarily for the raven-haired ones. He didn't need to see their faces. He would feel Mary before he saw her.

The crowd thinned away as he made his way closer to the water's edge. He could smell the stench of sewage and dead water, but continued on his path. There was no light here. He thought of the sea in Constanta, how it had been a great void in the night. He thought of how ready he was to enter that void.

"It's like the whole city disappeared, dontcha think?" a soft voice rang through the darkness.

He turned, but could see nothing.

"Who's there?"

"It's like the dark just swallowed 'er whole."

He began to tremble.

"Mary? Is it you?"

"I had a feelin' you'd come callin'."

"I asked for you. No one knew where you were. No one knew you."

"No one's ever known me."

Still, he could not see her.

"Let's move away from the banks, into the light. I wish to see you."

"Do you, then?"

"Yes, of course…Mary, what is it? You sound different."

"I didn't want you to see me like this. It comes and goes, you know. I was hopin' it would be gone when I seen you again."

"Mary, you're frightening me. Please come here."

"Oh, Mister Mille'ovo," she sighed. "I didn't want it to be this way."

"*God dammit, Mary*. Stop with this nonsense and show yourself to me!"

"You wanna see me? You wanna *really* see me?"

An extinguished gaslight flared above him and he was abruptly hit by a strong, fetid wind. The girl rushed toward him through the darkness and stopped in one fluid movement. A gash ran along her neck, deep and wide, from ear to ear. It glistened and wept, then poured like a scarlet waterfall down the front of her dress.

"Mary…my god." He thought he might be sick.

130

"I'm sorry you 'ave to see me like this, but you made it so."

He sobbed and shook his head. "No. Please, no."

"You got to mind yourself, me love. Don't lose yourself in your guilt or sorrow or you'll not see 'im coming."

He raised his head. "Who?"

She smiled sadly and said, "Death, lover." Blood pooled at her feet, and she glanced down and sighed. "Dreadful, innit?"

"Ivo. Is it Ivo?"

"No, you poor fool," she laughed. "It's the other half of Veda. The half you didn't destroy."

❧

We arrived in Martinique mostly unscathed. It had not been an easy journey, but you were far too young to have been affected by it. Your mother was rightfully unhappy from the moment we set foot on the ship, but a sense of peace seemed to fall over her once we entered the calmer, bluer waters of the Caribbean. She did not say much as we made our way through the port, but I could tell that in coming to the island I'd finally made a decision that pleased her. I cannot be certain, but I think, in that moment, she may have even smiled.

I wanted to smile, as well, but that I had no plan for us weighed on me as we wandered through the port. I did my very best to maintain the illusion that we would be fine. You cannot possibly imagine how desperately I wanted that to be true.

❧

They found a small café near the port where Veda could rest from the long journey while Vladimir collected his thoughts. He stared helplessly at his beautiful wife as she let the sea breeze move through her like a ghost. His child sat

131

quietly, happily sucking on a piece of crystallized sugar. It would have been a perfect moment had he only known what to do next.

He excused himself, fully aware of his intentions, despite the consequences. Just one drink. Just to set him straight.

Rum was the spirit of choice in this exotic place, and Vladimir wondered if the entire island might be made of sugar. There was nothing so sweet in Moscow. He ordered a drink from the Creole in the café keeping his back to his family, hoping they would not see.

"Michel," said a well-dressed man in a white suit sitting nearby to the black man serving the drinks, "that one is on me." He smiled at Vladimir and lit a cigar.

Vladimir smiled uneasily and nodded his head. "*Merci.*"

"My pleasure, good sir. If I may be so bold, you look like a gentleman in need of something to lighten the spirit."

"You must have known me for some time, then," Vladimir said with a slight grin.

"Yes, well, for all the pieces of you that I don't know, I *do* know a heavy heart when I see one." The man puffed on his cigar, savouring the sweetness. "Now, from where have you and your lovely family come, and what ghosts have you brought with you?"

Vladimir put his glass to his lips, thinking of what to say. The gentleman smiled and waited patiently, smoke drifting around him as though he were a great white dragon.

"We have come from many places, but most recently Algiers."

"Ah, I have been to that part of the world, but not Algeria. Not yet."

"It…eh…was nice enough for the likes of me, but not quite suitable for my wife and child."

"You are not French. Your French is quite good, but your accent betrays you," the white dragon laughed.

Vladimir looked down, slightly ashamed. "No, I was born in Moscow."

"That would have been my guess, *comrade.*"

Vladimir smiled and glanced around uncomfortably.

"And your ghosts?"

"They come from Moscow, as well."

The gentleman laughed quietly and stood to formally greet his new friend.

"My name is Étienne Grégoire, and I'd be honoured if you, your family, and *fantômes* would allow me to open my home to you after what was undoubtedly an arduous journey."

"That is much too kind, Monsieur Grégoire."

"That is how we do things here, *comrade. Bienvenue en Martinique.*"

Étienne Grégoire made his fortune the way most affluent people made their fortunes in the Antilles~ sugarcane. I remember his plantation home so well. It was hidden in a lush grove of palms, a piece of the French countryside that evolved over the years inside the jungle like an undiscovered species of butterfly. The island had taken its toll on the estate, but the salt and storm damage only served to give everything it brutalized an air of mystery and ancient beauty. Strange, how a scar in just the right place can be so captivating, so lovely, yet still remain a scar.

We had spent only mere moments at Étienne's estate, yet I could tell by the expression on your mother's beautiful, tired face that, for the first time since Constanta, she felt at home.

We dined with our new friend in his enchanting manor home and when it was done, we joined him in a tropical garden just below the second-story veranda. We talked for many hours, and he taught your mother how to say 'Bougainvillea', which for some time remained her favourite word. She smiled every time it fell from her lips.

I remember how you laughed as I brushed your tiny cheek with a bit of Spanish moss. I remember thinking that somehow, this island ~Étienne's home,

133

specifically~ might serve as a fortress against my ghosts. I remember how the sunset that evening lasted longer than I'd ever seen.

⤳

In some ways, Vladimir's hopes were realized. He didn't feel the presence of Ivo, nor the ghost of Katya. And for a few days, he wasn't suffocated by his own conscience. Before then, he couldn't remember the last time he really breathed, but now, here he was—*free*.

From the veranda he could see the ocean. Everything was so far away now. Algiers, Moscow, Constanta, Luca—everything. Even his demons.

Étienne Grégoire quickly became more than just a gracious host. He was a tutor to Veda, who desperately tried to understand all of the conversations around her. At one time, Vladimir always remembered that his language was not hers, and would speak slowly and clearly. She had loved him very much for that. But now, Vladimir was so consumed with his ills that he spoke the way strangers would speak to her, as though he was unaware that she was not native. It was Étienne who spoke carefully and with her interest at heart. It was Étienne that instructed his servants to do the same, as their thick Creole was even more difficult to understand. And it was Étienne that spent time with her daily, in the garden, helping her with her French, teaching her the language of the people of Martinique.

The wealthy Frenchman quickly endeared himself to young Ana as well, forever offering up trinkets and baubles for her entertainment, but it was Vladimir whom he took the greatest interest in. He would watch him constantly, studying him, dissecting him. What a strange, exotic creature this Russian was, and Monsieur Étienne did, indeed, love strange and exotic creatures.

He loved them enough to collect them, in fact. He'd had the good fortune to travel the world, and had seen many unusual things in his time, so when something really intrigued him, *truly* surprised him, Étienne Grégoire paid attention.

And how proud he was of his curiosities. Every day he had something new to show his guests, and for every artefact, every rare animal part, every ancient, mysterious thing, he had a story to tell along with it.

There were ornate feathers, and flora, and insects under glass unlike any Vladimir had ever seen. There were jewels and bones and ritualistic daggers. Obscure instruments and velvet chairs that once belonged to kings. The ragged and worn robes of holy men and the armour of long-dead warriors. Books bound in the flesh of trophy stags and the framed hides of beloved prize horses. Preserved creatures from the deepest ends of the sea, and unrecognisable body parts of supposed martyrs.

"This, my friend," he said to Vladimir as he placed a bowl in his hands, "this is the very bowl that was used by Caligula's winemaker. It is believed that the Emperor succumbed to lead poisoning after drinking wine for many years from this very piece. Which is to say that you are presently holding the instrument of Caligula's death," he smiled. "You can almost feel the imprint of the event, if you believe in that sort of thing. The way something so simple and innocuous can become sinister, yet its form remain unchanged. *If,*" he paused, expectantly, "you believe in that sort of thing."

He took the bowl from Vladimir and placed it in its home inside an oak cabinet.

"So tell me, friend," Étienne turned to face the Russian again and lit a cigarette. "*Do* you believe in that sort of thing?"

"I think it was their ignorance that wrought such tragedy. I think your bowl, while historically relevant, is by its nature, just a bowl."

Étienne smiled again, unaffected by Vladimir's rationale.

"Ah, I forget you are a scientist. Then may I show you something a bit more…diabolical?"

"Please."

The Frenchman crossed the room and removed a large knife from a glass case. He handed it to Vladimir as though it were a delicate orchid or a tiny bird.

135

"That is one of the many weapons that Gilles de Rais used to murder the children he sodomized."

Vladimir smiled uncomfortably, thinking for a moment that his host might have been joking, but Grégoire remained stoic.

"My god," Vladimir whispered.

"It's difficult to imagine such brutality, I know."

"I don't wish to hold it any longer. Please take it away." Vladimir offered the blade to his host, his hand shaking as he did so.

Étienne paused. "But, dear friend. This is, by its nature, only a knife. Quite possibly forged for no other purpose than hunting game. Why should it unnerve you so?"

Vladimir looked down and grinned. "Well played, sir."

Étienne smiled and took the knife from his hands and said, "It's not my first time."

Not everyone on the plantation was as fond of Vladimir as Étienne. In charge of the household were two sisters, Martine and Eulalie. They were Creoles, whom Étienne had found living on their own when they were only children. He knew they had come to Martinique with their family from the Seychelles, but little more. They were quiet girls, and would not say what became of their mother and father. At first, Étienne assumed they did not know, but as time went on and he began to understand the sisters better, he believed that they did, indeed, know the fate of their parents, but were unwilling to tell. Étienne, being a gentleman, did not press them. Whatever their secret, he surmised, it must be terrible, and this made the girls all the more mysterious to him.

He treated them very well, but it was no secret to anyone that Martine and Eulalie were, in his eyes, curiosities procured from the Seychelles. And what a lovely addition the pair made to his collection.

They took to Veda and Ana right away. They understood what it was to be in a strange land, the fear that comes in when familiarity is gone. They were grateful that at least they had some cousins here, and had deep empathy for Veda that—outside of the plantation—she had no one at all.

This was not so for Vladimir. They watched him the same way beaten dogs watch all men: with caution and suspicion. Vladimir may have shed his ghosts, but he could not shed the sickness within, and the sisters felt this. They felt things about people all the time, and they were almost never wrong.

Vladimir, in turn, was cordial, but was just as aware of the tension as they were. He thought them to be much like Veda's grandmother. They made him feel like a criminal, too. A devil.

But the sisters had a good arrangement with Étienne. They tolerated his eccentricities and he treated them very well, taking them in when they had nothing, allowing them to worship as they chose, and even employing their cousin Prosper and his brother-in-law Honoré, who desperately needed work. The sisters knew they would not find a better life anywhere else on the island, so they said nothing of their mistrust of their *Monsieur's* newest curiosity.

Veda could not have been happier with the sisters, with the way they fussed over Ana. She'd had no help with the child since leaving Constanta, and though she would never say it aloud, she was exhausted. The child, the journey across a sea that was larger than she ever could have imagined, learning a new language, all left her feeling spent. But nothing wore her down quite as much as her concern for her husband. He'd had some good days since they came to this place, but she knew it wouldn't be long until something dark crept in and tore apart their sense of calm.

The warm, salty days passed easily for Veda, the climate of the region not so different from that of her home in summer. Her French-Creole was improv-

137

ing every day, and Ana was thriving in what would be the first *home* she ever remembered. Veda liked that idea. It was a good home.

But while Veda enjoyed the life she never thought she'd have, the relationship between Étienne and Vladimir had taken on a strange form that did not go unnoticed by the sisters. Vladimir was drinking again, and the two would disappear for hours, almost nightly. The sisters were more than familiar with this behaviour, they'd seen *Monsieur* do it many, many times. They knew the sweet odour that drifted throughout the house very well, and they were used to the dream-like, nonsensical ravings of *Monsieur* that always followed. Now it seemed he'd found a companion in eccentricity. How unfortunate that his companion was prone to addiction and destruction, but this was something that Étienne would have had no way to know until it was upon them.

⚘

Veda believed in God. She also believed that common people could possess uncommon gifts that were traditionally bestowed upon angels and saints. She believed in the things she had seen her grandmother do. She believed in the things she'd done alone, and the things she'd done with Luca. And as the language barrier was broken down, she learned that Eulalie and Martine believed it, too.

The sisters practised a religion Étienne had referred to as *Voudoun*. They were the only servants they knew who were permitted to practice within their employer's household, and they revelled in that freedom.

They believed, at the heart of it, that God created heaven and earth, but was unattainable to man. Why should God be bothered with the petty ills of humans, or *moun* as the Creoles called them? So God, in his infinite wisdom created the *loa*; spirits, like demigods, who tended to the needs of *moun*. In exchange for this aid, *moun* had to make an offering or, during some rituals, be willing to be possessed. He would become a *cheval*—a horse—for the *loa* to ride. This was how the *loa* could best experience the pleasures of the flesh, and oh, how they loved those pleasures.

Veda was enchanted by this. The very thought of something so sublime entering a human body left her exhilarated and filled with curiosity. She had to know more, no matter what her husband might say. Rather fortunately for her, Vladimir spent much of his time in a haze, and didn't have much to say at all. Rather unfortunately for him, he was completely unaware of the state of his own family; Veda with her new religion, and Ana, now in her fourth year, speaking two languages and discovering the strange and beautiful world around her.

⟨≋⟩

Yet one more thing for which I cannot forgive myself. You were growing up two rooms away from me, and I never looked. By the time I opened my eyes, you were a person. You had ideas and opinions. You spoke like a young lady and you laughed at riddles. You had questions and the spark of desire, and I realized then that I did not know you at all. Your mother, with the help of Eulalie and Martine, had done a remarkable job bringing you up, and may I burn for never aiding her. May I burn for never telling her so.

⟨≋⟩

It was Martine that suggested Veda accompany her to Honoré's home. It was not very grand, but not so terrible for a man who tended Étienne's pigs and his small herd of goats. He lived there with his wife, Josephina, and her brother Prosper. Veda wondered immediately why she saw no children in the home, and as though she heard her thoughts, Martine quietly explained that despite their constant offerings, the *loa* had not yet granted them a child. Veda watched Honoré's wife during their visit and she knew just by the look in her eyes that Josephina carried the weight of their misfortune on her own. Her heart ached for the young woman, and she wondered whether Honoré chose to blame or comfort his barren wife. He *seemed* like a decent soul. She hoped, for Josephina, that was true.

139

When they were alone, Veda asked Martine if the *loa* were not so different than the Christian God, since they did not answer every prayer.

Martine said, "Oh, but they do. Just not always in the way you expect."

⤜

It did not take long for Veda, despite her ethnicity, to be welcomed into the *Société*. Between the mystery she carried with her as a stranger, and her warm and intuitive nature, some of the small community quickly believed her to be a Caucasian aspect of one of their *loa,* a spirit of love and prosperity called *Erzulie*, and Veda hungrily accepted this theory. She was made to feel at ease with the group—even special—except for with Josephina, who seemed distant from everyone, and for Josephina's brother, Prosper. Veda sensed he did not trust her, or trust the *Société's* assumption of her, though she meant no harm or disrespect. Perhaps Prosper would come to see this in time.

She adapted to their way of life just as quickly as they accepted her. There were times when it was difficult for her to decipher the conversations around her, but Martine or Honoré would always make sure she understood. Soon, she was spending more time in town with the *Société* than at the plantation. She was certain no one missed her.

But Ana did. Eulalie was good with the child, but Eulalie was not her mother. When she would see her father—which was rare—he always seemed so strange, so funny, but not like a jester. He did not seem aware that he was acting funny, and this frightened Ana a bit, but she enjoyed how sweet he always smelled and how, when he kissed her, his lips tasted of molasses. She missed her mother's smell. Soon, she would forget, as she'd once feared so long ago, in yet another foreign land.

⤜

Eulalie cared for the child deeply, and was protective of her when Vladimir would appear, enough so that Vladimir began to resent the young woman. It was hard enough being affectionate with his daughter with Veda looming over her like a lioness. He did not appreciate a servant doing the same. He would speak to Veda on this matter when he saw her, at which point he realized that he hadn't seen her in a rather long time.

He knew he'd heard her voice now and then, her laughter echoing through the house, but this was not a regular occurrence. Étienne tried to assure him that Veda was well, she had merely taken to the town, but Vladimir was not pleased with the thought of his wife cavorting around while an uneducated Creole raised his child. *What was she doing there? Who was she with? And what of Ana? Should their child be without her mother so often?* Étienne did not have adequate answers and Eulalie refused to talk.

"Where I come from, *Mademoiselle*, a servant does what she is told and does not withhold information from her master," Vladimir snapped.

Eulalie scooped Ana from the place she played on the kitchen floor and held her close. "*Oui, Monsieur Millerovo,* but we are not where you come from and you are not my master."

There were no pleasantries when Veda returned home that evening, and though his words were not loving or kind, she was taken by surprise that he had any words for her at all. Usually he was tucked away in the study with their host, or unconscious, or both.

"Where have you been?"

Veda paused and gazed upon him. She barely recognized him anymore. He'd never looked healthy, but now it was worse and she was disheartened by what she saw. She'd seen it before, in Moscow.

"I was in town, with Martine and her family. They're quite lovely— "

"I don't care if they're *royalty*," he snapped. "What do you mean by running off every day and leaving Ana with the servants?"

"When did you become so interested in what I do with Ana? You've never cared before."

"I should rap you across the mouth for that."

"Do it and you'll never see Ana or me again, I swear it." She narrowed her eyes and readied herself for what might come next.

But he only nodded his head slowly, staring her down with threatening, hateful eyes.

"I've seen you this way before, Vladimir," she continued. "I won't live that way again."

"I'm not the same person I was then," he said.

"That is the truth. You used to say you were sorry for being such a bastard."

London 1887

He was sick; sick to death of these ghosts, these murdered whores predicting his future, robbing him of his sanity like a band of abject thieves. Who were they to judge him for his crimes?

But they were right. They were always right. And so he knew that death was coming for him. Death and its companion, Vengeance. There was nothing he could do but wait. He only hoped there would be enough time for him to finish his letter to his daughter. Only then would he be ready.

In a dark, hidden pub, on the other side of the river, a young man, black-haired, beautiful, and damaged, sat alone below a dim gaslight with a drink in one hand and in the other, a tattered photograph of his beloved sister, looking strong and serene and standing next to the man who was responsible for her death. He knew exactly where to find him. He just needed his sister to tell him when it was time.

Martinique 1874

"Eulalie, who gave Ana this doll?" asked Veda, smiling at its delicate china face and smoothing out the fabric of its plain white dress. Its hair was black and silken, like Veda's own.

Eulalie looked up from her stitching. "Couldn't say, *Madame*. Perhaps *Monsieur*?"

"Perhaps. But Ana's birthday is not until Monday."

Eulalie smiled to herself. "I can't believe *Mademoiselle* is to be five already."

"Nor can I," Veda said softly, still gazing at the doll, entranced. She blinked hard, suddenly remembering herself, and placed the doll on the chair next to her. "I will see if *Monsieur* knows anything about this." She smiled and went to find Étienne.

But Étienne knew nothing of the doll. Nor did her husband, or Martine, or anyone else that came and went through the house.

She found Ana playing in the garden.

"I met your new friend today, Ana."

The little girl continued to play, saying nothing.

"Why is she not out here with you and your other dolls?"

Still, Ana did not look up. "They don't like her," she said flatly.

"Why is that?"

"She says bad things."

"What does she say?"

"Just bad things," Ana said, twirling one of the dolls in the air. "She sounds crazy and never makes any sense. We try to ignore her but then she will scream and scream. I wish she'd just leave. We all do."

"Ana, who gave her to you?"

"No one. I found her."

"You found her? And where was this?"

"Right here in the garden. But when we are playing here, she must stay inside. Then when we go inside, she must come out or else everyone will be mad and crying."

"Well, we certainly can't have that."

The little girl shook her head and carried on with her solitary game. Veda hoped her face hadn't betrayed her. She did not wish upon her child the fear she suddenly felt.

Veda could not bring herself to look at her husband, and she began to hate him for it. It was Moscow all over again, save for the cold, although this time she was not so alone. She had sisters now, and for that much she was grateful.

She'd been forthcoming about her past with Martine and, much to her surprise, with Honoré. He seemed to understand what it was to love someone who disappeared a little more each day. His wife Josephina seemed to be a hollow shell. With nothing inside, she was certain to break apart under the force of the waves, and Honoré was the kind of man who needed someone not so fragile.

"At times, I think it a blessing that she cannot bear children," Honoré confided in Veda one evening. "I fear she'd not survive it."

"Perhaps one day, when the time is right, she will be able."

"She isn't strong, Veda." He said her name so differently than Vladimir. It fell so heavily from her husband's lips that she almost didn't recognize it as her own when Honoré spoke it.

Bougainvillea.

Honoré stared at her hungrily and continued. "She isn't like you," he said.

She feared looking too deeply into his sleepy, black eyes, that she might never find her way home in such darkness.

Later that night, while she lay in bed alone, she dreamed of Honoré the same way she had once dreamed of Vladimir when he was still a stranger in Constanta.

It was the eve of Ana's birthday, yet her mother and father were nowhere in sight. Even at her young age, Ana saw the pattern emerge and knew that it was unlikely she'd be seeing much of either of them any time soon.

But *Monsieur* Étienne, with the assistance of Eulalie, had not forgotten. Ana squealed in delight when she saw what they had done to the parlour.

From the chandelier in the centre of the room, ribbons of every colour streamed down and around the furniture like a candied web, and at the end of each ribbon, hidden under tables or tucked away behind chairs, a gift. She couldn't imagine how she would ever make it through the night while such treasures awaited her, but *that,* Monsieur said, was part of the fun.

She was so entranced by it all that she did not notice when her father finally came stumbling in.

"Ana," he said, with the funny voice he sometimes used, "you should take better care with your dolls. I found this one outside." He presented the black-haired doll to her, squeezing it roughly around the waist.

She turned to face him. He was so tall and unsteady and strange, but she knew in her belly that she should never act afraid before him.

"That's where she's meant to be right now."

"So when someone is kind enough to give you a gift, you leave it outside to the rain and the insects?"

She hated when he spoke in the funny voice. All of his words ran together like one.

"*Oui,* Papa. We don't want her here."

145

"Well," he scoffed, "perhaps I should take her into town and give her to some other child who is not so spoiled as you."

"You can if you want. But it won't matter," she said, unblinking. She would not cower or cry.

"And why is that?"

Ana looked at him and sighed with exasperation. "Because, Papa, she'll be right back here again tomorrow."

∾

It was not far from his home that same night, in an abandoned one-room house near the beach, but hidden in a small grove of palms, that Honoré took Veda without hesitation. He grabbed her around the waist and flung her around, the way Vladimir had done with the doll. They grunted and struggled and put their gaping mouths on each other until Veda was gasping for air, and scraping her nails on the rough, splintered wooden floor they lay upon.

But it was not the image of this that terrified Ana as she closed her eyes to sleep. It was the horrific creature that stood in the shadows as her mother and the dark man play-fought on the floor of the weather-beaten shack. Its body was that of a man, but its head was a horse, skinned and raw and bleeding, and Ana knew that it meant to devour them.

∾

Try as she might, Eulalie could do nothing to calm the screaming child as she tore at her covers and her nightgown. She prayed the men might hear and come to her aid, but Vladimir did not stir. Étienne eventually appeared in the doorway of Ana's room, but only seemed confused by the scene before him.

Eulalie supposed that, in his haze, he thought he might be dreaming, which rendered him useless to her.

"What's all this now, Eula?"

"*Mademoiselle* is ill, *Monsieur*! She's having a fit!"

"My, oh, my, how I understand." He held on to the doorframe to steady himself. "You just let it all out, *ma petite*. Until you're old enough to partake in spirits, it's the only way to make it stop." He sauntered down the hall, lazily shaking his head and muttering to himself.

Eulalie wrapped her arms around Ana and fell onto the bed, restraining the girl under her own weight. She hoped Martine and Veda were enjoying themselves in town while the tiny creature in her arms was falling apart. Something in the air was stirring, Eulalie knew, and the coming tempest wasn't going to be merciful, neither for the guilty nor the innocent.

Though she could hear the sisters talking, the pace at which they spoke was so rapid that Veda could not understand as she listened at the kitchen door. She was sick over what had happened to Ana while she was away, and wanted nothing more than to understand it. Her child was, at last, resting, but torn to pieces at her own delicate hand. She could not imagine what had scared Ana so badly that she would harm herself in the wake of it.

She stood at the door quietly, struggling to comprehend the discussion, when Eulalie opened it without warning, nearly causing Veda to fall.

"Come in, instead of hiding at the door like a mouse waiting for the cat to leave." Veda blushed, most of the colour hidden by her olive complexion, and said she was sorry, but only wanted to understand what had happened to her child.

"She dreamed, *Madame*. But not like you dream. She dreamed what is real. She dreamed what is coming."

"Are you saying she had a premonition?"

"*Oui, Madame*. I believe she did."

"How do you know this?"

147

"She saw something she never should have seen."

"What?"

"She saw you sin. And she saw what you will suffer."

Veda stiffened. "I have not sinned."

"It is no matter to me, *Madame*. I'm not the one judging."

"*Madame*," Martine said quietly, "you told me once you have brothers. Tell us, is one of them your twin?"

"*Oui*, my brother Luca. How did you know?"

"Because where there are twins, there's almost always a *gift*," Martine replied.

"But sometimes it's not such a gift, but a curse," Eulalie said.

"You believe my daughter to be cursed? What a terrible thing to say!" Veda cried.

"If she is cursed, it is only by your doing, *Madame*," Eulalie said calmly. "You can change your path at any time."

But Veda did not change her path. She continued to see Honoré under the cover of darkness, and she continued to avoid Vladimir. She found it difficult to be alone with Ana. Her only child was not like her, and she, not like her child. If she had a spark of intuition inside of her, then Ana had raging fire, and this frightened her. It also did something she hadn't expected—it made her terribly jealous. Honoré and some of the others had made her feel special, but she paled in comparison to her daughter. Even to be *cursed* with such an ability was better than not having it at all, or so Veda believed.

It was a ridiculous thing—to be jealous of a child. What could Ana know of the world? To be sure, she was an unusual little girl, but she'd had an unusual life; always moving, always meeting new people, living with an unstable father and all the tension he wrought. These were things that would undoubtedly affect a grown person, let alone a small child. It was not a spirit, nor a gift, nor a curse that gave Ana terrible dreams. It was her own intensity. And those dreams were not premonitions, but the colourful imaginings of a child who'd seen more in her precious few years than most people see in a lifetime. And if Ana *was* indeed *touched*, it was *certainly* inherited from Veda's kin, and it was *certainly* not nearly as strong as it had been in generations past. A ridiculous thing, indeed.

Veda contented herself with her reasoning as she moved silently through the house and out into the garden, without plan or purpose. Surveying the beautiful surroundings, her thoughts turned to Honoré and she smiled to herself, her body suddenly full of warmth and electricity. She was lost, drifting through the gossamer hazy mist that rose from the dense foliage in humid air, entranced by the heavy scent of earth and honey, and would have been content to stay there had it not been for the doll.

She hadn't seen it when she came out, but now, here it was, lying in the middle of the path for anyone to trip over. It made her angry to see it there, and she would be sure to scold Ana for it later. It was one thing if the child didn't want to play with it, but another to leave it underfoot, as though it were someone else's problem. If she wasn't careful, that child was going to grow up to be as inconsiderate as her father, never caring about the messes they left for everyone else to clean up; the weight put upon everyone else's shoulders. She'd be damned if he was going to influence their daughter that way. She'd sooner see them all dead rather than raise a selfish, miserable—

What was she thinking? Her eyes filled with tears as she heard her own words echo through her head in three languages, and she was suddenly awash with shame. How could she have gotten so angry, her thoughts turned so poisonous, over a toy? It was the stress of things, to be sure. Even here in paradise, her life was still so chaotic.

She wiped her face with the back of her hand and picked up the doll. Immediately, the tears came flooding back and she gasped, swallowing hard to keep from being overheard.

"What is wrong with you?" she whispered harshly to herself, almost laughing at the absurdity of it all. "Stop it. Just stop it right now."

Was she talking to herself or to the doll?

She pulled a tiny leaf from the doll's long, black hair, and smoothed it down. She wiped a bit of dirt from the white dress and smoothed it down, as well.

"See? You aren't so terrible, are you? You just need a little kindness and care. Maybe if Ana doesn't want to play with you then you can stay with me, *oui*?"

Veda continued to preen the doll, putting herself at ease as she did. A thin red thread was wound around the doll's fragile neck. Something from one of Ana's dresses, Veda imagined. She carefully pulled at it, to loosen and unwind it, but it would not come. Her fingers were that of a weaver's, used to working in small and delicate spaces, and it should have been nothing to undo the thread, but it seemed that the harder she tried, the worse the tangle became.

"Come, now…I could snap you right off…"

The thread seemed to be thickening, knotting itself worse and worse.

"Really, now. I don't understand how…"

Less and less of the doll's neck remained visible, the thread now appearing to have no discernible ends. Veda scoffed, frustrated and confused, her brow moist and her fingers shaking and sore. How could her fingers be sore? She was a weaver down to her bones. She was overcome with anger again. Here, she'd tried to take care of the doll and this was her thanks. No wonder Ana hated it so much. But this was how it was. You work so hard to care for something and it just eats you alive. Sometimes, Veda thought, it might be better just to tear everything apart and start anew. Better to destroy now that which would destroy you later—

"My *God*!" Veda cried out. "What is wrong with you?" she screamed at the doll, shaking it violently.

"Madame?"

The voice, although soft and calm, startled Veda and she dropped the doll to the ground.

"Eulalie…I'm sorry. I…"

"No apologies, Madame. It has been a long day."

Eulalie's voice, even and almost hypnotic, implied to Veda that she needn't explain.

"Yes," Veda replied quietly, her face streaked with tears and creased with confusion. "It has been a terribly long day."

Veda stepped over the doll with caution, and Eulalie led her inside.

For the first time since the sister could recall, she locked the garden door behind them.

Ana was terrified. It was one thing when the doll said such horrible things, but now, this dreadful messenger was inside of her, and no one could make it go away, not even Eulalie. Everything was different now. Things weren't as beautiful as they had once been, and there was nowhere that the red horse couldn't find her. She tried so hard to explain it to Eulalie, but of course, it didn't make sense. There was no such creature and Ana couldn't understand why she kept dreaming, sometimes even when she was awake, about this beast. Ana couldn't understand why it was that every time she saw her mother, she felt sick and the air felt like when a storm was coming.

She once loved to play with the goats, but she could not go near them anymore. They were afraid of her. And, save for Eulalie and Martine, so were the servants. Even her father, whom she rarely saw, acted strangely in her presence. Then again, her father always acted strangely. But it was the change in the way her mother looked upon her that made her the saddest. Her mother had always kept her safe, but now she was opening the gates and letting all the monsters in as though it didn't matter at all.

Vladimir wandered in a haze through the lush garden beyond the house and down the hill to the place where the goats and pigs were kept. It was not yet noon, but the sun already broke through the canopy, warming all it touched to a slightly uncomfortable degree. The thickness of the air captured the sweet, earthen scents of the surrounding flora and made for a strangely pleasant feeling of suffocation, until he came too near to the animal pens. The odour of the beasts hung in the air, heavier than the hibiscus ever could.

A man carrying two pails came from a small, weather-beaten shack and hopped the fence. The goats scattered playfully as he shooed them away from their feed trough.

Vladimir knew the man but could not remember his name.

The man emptied his pails into the trough and nodded cautiously at the tall stranger.

"I don't envy your work, man," Vladimir said.

"It is honest work," the man replied in thick Creole and gave the Russian a deliberate glance.

"What is your name?" Vladimir asked.

"Prosper."

"That is quite an unusual name."

"Not here," Prosper said, not looking at the Russian. "Here," he paused, "yours is an unusual name."

"You know my name?"

"Oui, Monsieur Millerovo."

Vladimir raised an eyebrow in surprise.

"It is my job to know who *Monsieur* Étienne brings to this place," Prosper continued.

"Is that so? I thought it was a servant's job to know only what his master wishes."

"Oui. And *Monsieur* Étienne wishes me to know who he brings to this place."

Vladimir laughed quietly. "So, you possess some ability to know your master's guests better than he?"

"He is not my *master,* as you say. He is my employer. And sometimes, yes, I *do* know his guests better than he."

"Well, now I am intrigued." Vladimir came closer to the fence as the goats vied for the best positions at the trough.

Prosper did not look at, nor respond to, the Russian.

"So, what do you know of me?"

"It's not for me to speak of such things, *Monsieur*."

"But I am inquiring. Surely you would not deny me what I wish."

Prosper turned and faced the stranger.

"You do not truly wish to know what I see in you."

"Now, you see…if you could truly see into me, you'd know that I do."

"Tell yourself what you must. That is your way, *non*?"

Vladimir held the man's gaze, at once feeling sick, crushed by the weight of the air around him.

"You want to speak of vision, *Monsieur*?" Prosper continued, moving closer to the Russian. "I will tell you something of vision…"

"What's that?"

"You have none."

"You take care what you say, man."

"Should I only tell you what I see if it will appeal to you? Should I lie?"

Vladimir swallowed hard, but said nothing.

"You blind yourself every day to what surrounds you, what surrounds your little child."

"What do you know of it, when you are out here reeking in the heat with these filthy beasts?"

"I know you numb yourself because you do not like what dwells inside you. But I also know that when you do it, you miss too much."

"I am astounded at your implication. I'm sure your master will be none too pleased to know of this conversation."

Prosper shrugged. "Surely, *Monsieur*, I could not deny you what you wished."

Vladimir trembled with anger. "We will speak of this later…at the house."

"*Oui, Monsieur*. And when you wish to see the truth, you know where to find me. I'll be right here, reeking with my beasts."

London, 1887

Luca stood silently before the innkeeper, holding strange coins in his open palm. His hand was shaking, not because of what he planned to do—there was nothing but resolve in that—but because he was nervous to use what little English he'd learned during his travels. He'd already been turned away by one innkeeper who thought he was a gypsy, and now he was exhausted and wanted only to rest and wait for his twin to speak to him once again.

And speak, she did. When the second innkeeper denied him a bed—*no room, no room,* he'd shouted, as though he would better understand if he spoke in a louder voice—Luca found himself wandering the streets, lost and alone. It was a strange, violent wind that blew up from the river on the otherwise windless night that carried her back to him. There were no words, but the sudden storm that drove Luca into yet another inn could not have come from anything other than his sister, and though he had little money to spare, he felt compelled by her to take a seat at the bar and order a drink.

"Ain' seen the likes of you before, friend," the small, pale man he sat next to said.

But Luca did not understand.

"Ah, I see. You ain' local. Where you from?"

Luca knew this. He knew *where* and *you* and *from*. "Constanta," he said, pleased with himself.

"Con-stan-sea-ah?" the pale man said it so oddly. "That sounds far away from here. Where is 'at?"

Where again. "Romania."

"Oh-ho! A gypsy!"

Luca knew this, too. "No, no, *no!*" he said, disturbed by such an assumption.

"A' ight, a' ight…settle yourself, man," the pale man laughed.

"No gypsy," Luca said, just to be clear.

"No gypsy," the pale man nodded in agreement, smiling widely with his little rat teeth. "Wha's your name?"

Luca smiled, relieved to have understood once again. "Luca," he paused, remembering what he and Veda had decided so long ago. "Luca Estela."

The pale man extended his boney hand and said slowly, "Charmed. My name is Lloyd Pinkney."

⚘

Oh, Ana, I was such a fool. Worse than a fool. I was mad with addiction, but of course could not see that for myself. Had you the words, you might have told me, made me see what a wretched creature I'd become, but you were so small and innocent, and while your mother was consumed by her lover, I was consumed by pain and fear and madness. But the very worst thing I allowed to consume me was rage. It is because of that rage that we find ourselves here, drowning in this fate.

⚘

Ana sat in the garden. She had always been happy there. The stone pathway was perpetually cool, shaded by the canopy of tall, giant-leafed plants, perfect for shielding her from the great, big sun. But today she did not feel well. Today, everything was wrong.

None the less, she played with her dolls, trying her very best to pretend that everything was *not at all* wrong. Perhaps she could pretend that today was a different sort of day. She closed her eyes tightly and breathed out hard. When she opened them, it was still today, worse than before. The exiled doll lay among the others, as though it had been there all along.

Ana was infuriated. She had never hated anything as much as she hated this doll, and doubted she ever would. But she believed when it said that it would always find its way back to her, just as she believed when it said that something terrible was coming, and that it would come on the back of the red horse. That dreadful red horse that made her burn inside. It filled her with shame and fear, and it showed her ugly pictures that she wished she had not seen, pictures of things she did not understand and could barely speak of. She had always loved horses, but now everything was different. She didn't think she loved much at all, anymore.

She picked up the doll and stared right into its dead eyes, and though she knew it would do no good, she threw it against the wall of the house with all of her strength, tears of rage streaming from her eyes as it shattered and fell to the ground. She collected her good dolls and ran into the house, crying and calling for Eulalie. She did not see the tiny, broken human bones that spilled out of its broken china body on the ground, but as she suspected, by the next morning, the doll was back, healed and whole, waiting for its mistress.

Vladimir sat quietly in Étienne's study, swirling his drink and staring blankly at the wall.

Étienne smiled at him kindly. "What troubles you, my boy?"

"Your servant. Prosper."

"And how does Prosper trouble you?" the Frenchman asked, lighting his pipe.

Vladimir immediately relaxed upon smelling the pipe.

"I believe him to be duplicitous. He leads me to believe he knows something important about my family and myself, yet when I demand he reveal such information, he refuses," he watched the smoke swirl from the pipe, nearly hypnotized by its essence.

"I should think he knows nothing at all and is playing some sort of game with me, one that I do not appreciate."

"Ah, *oui*. Prosper is a very strong-willed man. He can, at times, be secretive and difficult to communicate with, but I have never known him to be a liar. I assure you, I would not keep a untrustworthy person in my employ."

"Then what is it he could possibly know about us?"

Étienne offered the pipe to the Russian.

"Perhaps it is not one specific, tangible thing. Perhaps it is something to do with feelings and intentions."

"Perhaps. I suppose I'm not used to being spoken to so presumptuously by a servant."

"And you've had many servants…back in Moscow?"

Vladimir paused, then said, "No, I did not," as crimson filled his cheeks. "I may have forgotten myself. Forgive me."

"No need for that, friend. Perhaps as time goes on, you will trust my judgement in household matters."

"Indeed, I will."

"And so you understand, these people are not my *servants*, as you say. Those dark days are over. They are my employees, and in some ways, the closest family I've ever had. Along with you and yours, of course." He smiled, but there was sadness in his eyes.

"I understand. I truly do," Vladimir humbly replied.

Smoke veiled his face and suddenly, he did not care so much about any of it.

Veda and Martine sat in Josephina's cramped and sweltering kitchen, talking and watching Josephina as she sorted through several small piles of dried herbs, sweeping them in their designated canisters with delicate fingers. Tiny beads of perspiration collected on her full upper lip, but she dare not wipe them away, lest she contaminate the herbs with her own impurities, rendering them useless in rituals. It wasn't really the heat, but the presence of Veda that made her sweat. She couldn't help but notice that the woman was barely affected by the hot, humid air. She finally spoke, joining in on the conversation, but would not look her guest in the eye.

"You do not mind the heat? I thought it was cold where you came from," she said softly.

"In Moscow, *oui*, it was very cold. But in my home—Constanta—it is very warm. I miss it so," Veda replied.

Josephina cleared her throat. "Why don't you go back, then?"

Martine's eyes widened. "Jo! Really, now!"

"It was only a question. I meant no harm."

"It's fine, Martine," Veda said, casting her eyes down. "Were it my choice, I *would* go home. But my husband…"

Josephina cut in, "…he doesn't fit there, *non*?"

"*Non*. I don't think he will ever let us return."

"I should think he doesn't have much say over what you do. Not with you spending so much time here, away from your family," Josephina replied.

Veda swallowed hard, clearly taken aback by Josephina's change in demeanour.

"Things are…troubled…for us," Veda said shamefully. "It's better that I spend my time here, away from home."

"Better for whom?" Josephina quipped, brushing her hands free of the tiny bits of herbs.

"*Josephina!*" Martine hissed.

"No, Martine. She is only speaking her mind. And this is her home, after all."

"Honoré and I have our troubles as well, but I won't find the answer by running away. The shadows that follow us are our own. We can never outrun them. That's what I know."

"Then you know more than I," Veda said.

"Perhaps, *Madame*, but some days, I wish I didn't."

Veda met with Honoré later that night with a mixture of shame and spite in her heart. Josephina knew their secret. Of this, Veda was certain, yet she could not forgive the delicately venomous way Honoré's wife had spoken to her. Veda possessed gifts that Josephina did not, and in the future would insist that she be treated with the respect she deserved.

Although, deep in her troubled heart, she knew she had.

It did not make sense, the fire that burned within her for this man—a man she barely knew—but it was undeniably real, blazing its way through her, devastating everything in its path like the intentional fires she'd seen in the fields.

There was a spark between them, to be sure, but there must be a kind of passion that rises from a painful common bond, she reasoned. It is quick and strong as though it must somehow atone for past failures; guilty of making you fall in love and bind yourself to one who would abandon you—if not in body, then in spirit. But now, here it is, offering you another chance, offering you an open window. How could you not climb through?

Her love for Honoré seemed to grow with every passing hour. True, he was her window, but no more than she was his. There would be time to reveal themselves to each other once they were free. They could be whomever they wished. They could wash their former lives away in the sea.

It was a journey she had never been able to take with Vladimir. Not with his secrets and lies. Not with his addictions. She knew *what* he was when she left Romania with him—just as her grandmother had said in her stories—and she knew he would never be anything else. No matter how many windows, he would never be free.

Vladimir spent the night in a haze, once again unaware that his wife had not come home until the early morning hours. And it was in the early morning hours that he stepped quietly, unnoticed, into the doorway of the bedroom that he no longer shared with her and watched her as she undressed. He could not remember the last time he saw her naked. She looked different than he remembered, like she was no longer part of him.

"Where were you?" he asked softly.

She quickly turned and covered herself with her skirt.

"I didn't hear you come in," she said.

"I can see that." He leaned against the doorframe and gazed at her. "But I asked you a question."

"I was in town. With Martine."

"Does Martine even work here anymore? It seems the two of you are always *in town* together." His voice remained calm.

"That is a matter between Martine and *Monsieur* Étienne," she replied, still clutching her underskirt to her chest.

"And what of the matter between you and me?" He moved further into the room.

"And what matter would that be?" She could not look at him.

He came closer still and took her gently by the shoulders. "The matter of our marriage? The matter of how I can't remember the last time I touched you? The matter of how you disappear for all hours of the night and leave me in the dark? Are any of these matters important to you, Veda?"

"They were…once," she kept her eyes down. "But you seem to forget the matter of your constant drinking and your *medicines*. And the matter of how you forget you even have a wife and child. And the matter of your temper. What of these matters, husband?"

"I forget I have a wife because she is little more than a ghost that slips through the house as the sun rises. I forget I have a child because she is kept from me, *monster* that I am, by that superstitious coloured woman. I drink and smoke because I have nothing else in this place. And I am angry *because* of these things."

"And in Moscow? And Algiers? When Ana and I were there each and every day, waiting for you, praying you were not dead in the street? What was your excuse then?"

He let her go and took a step back. "Look at me, Veda."

She raised her eyes and forced back tears.

"We have *both* been monsters. We are *both* crushed by the weight of our failings and our shame. I can say this. I know that it does not absolve me, but I can *say* it. Can you?"

Her tears fell. "You used to think I was perfect."

"You were." His face fell. "And then I broke you."

"Then how can you call *me* a monster?" She buried her face in her skirt.

"Because you chose to remain broken, my love. Just like I did."

He turned and walked away.

I'd hoped I'd gotten through to her in some small way, but she carried on with her secret life as though I'd never mentioned it. I knew in my heart that every-thing was my fault, but I also knew that it would take both of us to mend our little world. Though I cannot blame her for it, your mother seemed past the point of no return by then. I would give anything now to have been able to accept this and act accordingly, with your best interest at heart, but I was out of my head and infuri-ated by her unwillingness to reconcile with me. I may have deserved every bit of it, but pain is still pain, and it can make you do desperate, unspeakable things.

The staff were at odds. Martine and Eulalie argued constantly, seemingly over everything, but mostly over Ana and her absent mother. Prosper barely spoke to Honoré anymore, and when he did it was cold and resentful. Veda knew this was her doing, but was tangled in too tightly to see a way out. She was in love with Honoré and there was nothing more to be said about it. But she did not have a plan. She could leave Vladimir, but he would never allow a civil separation. She would have to take Ana and disappear. And if she did, would Honoré leave his wife and follow her? And where would they go? The island seemed smaller every day and suddenly, her window did not seem to be opened so wide.

She prayed and made offerings to her new gods, in desperate need of an answer, but nothing clear ever came through. Her heart only led her back to Honoré, but somewhere else within her, a terrible, relentless burning had begun and would not cease. Sometimes, she would wake suddenly, drenched with her own sweat and tears, and for the first few moments, everything was red. Images of her infidelities would flash before her like some horrible magic, and *god*, how they burned. Everything in her burned. She would sit before her mirror and watch as her face contorted in a monstrous way, into something she could not recognize. And in those moments, she could feel an unknown presence behind her, waiting, ready to consume her when the time was right. It fed on guilty hearts and fire and every other hateful thing inside one's soul. Then she would weep, put her trembling hands to her head, and beg it to take her. But it never would.

She dreamed, guiltily, of her brother. They were in the caves on the shores of her beloved Black Sea, and he held her tightly, pleading with her to stay, grasping at her arms and her head, kissing her tear-stained face. *You don't have to do this,* he cried. *The world is yours, you don't have to end,* he whispered, but she did not understand. She pulled away and walked out of the cave into the sunlight, but the sea was gone. All that remained was a deep, arid canyon. Luca came to the edge, crying once again, but she could not stay.

The sea has always been there, and it is there, still...only now I see it has changed. She was so certain, certain enough to step from the edge and let herself fall. But as she fell, she could see that the sea had not returned, and she burned with the shame of her foolishness as she plummeted to the red rocks below.

≫

In another place, Ana was having nightmares of her very own. So frequently, in fact, that Eulalie had taken to sleeping in a chair next to the child's bed, so when she woke up screaming, she would not be all alone.

She wanted so badly to tell Eulalie what she saw at night. She wanted to tell her about the china doll, everything, but at five years old, she simply did not have the words. To say she dreamt a horse monster and it was frightening was not enough. It was so much worse than that, but she did not know a word that was worse than frightening. Instead, she painted pictures.

When she asked for some pens and paper, *Monsieur* Étienne said that simple pens and paper would never do, and gave her a set of beautiful watercolours. She was grateful, but saddened that she would have to paint such horrible things with *Monsieur's* lovely gift. But she needed them to know.

She asked *Monsieur* to help her outline a horse, which he did. And she asked if there was a way to make the pale red pigment darker, like apples or blood, and he showed her. And when it was done, she knew he'd tried his very best to pretend he was not upset by what he saw.

≫

Josephina had never been a hateful, vengeful woman, not by her own choice, anyway. But over so much time, she'd grown weary of the constant battle in her head. The *loa* had long ignored her pleas and offerings for peace, for quiet, and she had no choice but to believe that it was a curse upon her heart. Not a curse laid upon her by another living person, but one she had been born with, perhaps as a punishment for the sins of her ancestors; perhaps as a punishment for some crime committed, in the aether, by her soul from a time before she could remember. Whatever the reason, it damned her to be alone, no matter who might be near. It damned her heart to be abandoned by her husband, and her womb abandoned by God. There was no one for her to care for: no children, no life force, nothing to look forward to. She'd grown so weary, in fact, that she did not protest when her husband left night after night to be with his black-haired, pallid-skinned horse; so beautiful on the outside, but so very ugly within. His wretched, spoiled rag doll who cared so little for her own child that she should leave her in the darkest hours to be raised by strangers, and *oh*, what Josephina would have done to trade lives with her. So many times, as the vapid interloper sat in their home, laughing and drinking their spirits, drinking in their traditions and beliefs, her eyes wide like a child's, waiting for her lapdogs to so carefully explain every little thing, every simple word she did not know—she wanted to scream at her. The way Martine and Josephina's own faithless dog of a husband flocked to her and coddled her—she just wanted to smack her flawless face and say, *"Go! Take my husband. Take what family I have and leave your child, and I will make sure she does not grow up to be a shallow, vacant puppet like her mother! I will pay her mind, I will give her the attention you cannot! I will help her learn to cherish her gift, rather than suffer it alone. Just take the dogs and go!"*

But that would never happen. Veda would have *everything* except the understanding of how precious everything she had truly was. Josephina was not an educated woman, but she knew this much was true.

She had not made the doll to harm or frighten the child, but it was only through the child that her will could be done. The doll was a seed, the beginnings of a poisonous, parasitic vine that would grow and seek out the host it desired, consuming her. The child would bring the seed into their home, and though only Ana would hear her words and know her intentions, Josephina knew the fastest way to the mother's heart would be through her child. The girl was plagued by the terrible gift of vision already, Josephina reasoned. Certainly, this would be a mere grain of sand in the vast open wound that was Ana's psyche.

It was more than petty jealously. Josephina had—for so very long—a poisonous seed of her own buried in her heart, in need of a heavy rain to bring it to life. And now the rain had come, from far across the ocean, carrying with it a despicable creature somehow blessed by the same spirits who had shunned Josephina her whole wretched life, despite her dedication. Josephina wondered if that creature would have any idea of the destruction she would cause.

"Tell me what happens when my wife goes to the town. Do you see her?" Vladimir asked, as the small herd of goats nipped at his fingertips in search of food. He hated the pens, but if he was to learn anything from Prosper, he knew he'd have to go to him.

"I do. She comes to my sister's home."

"Is she close to your sister?"

"No," Prosper said flatly. "She's close to my brother-in-law, Honoré."

Vladimir clenched his fists. He knew the answer to his next question without asking, but he wanted to hear it anyway.

"How close?"

Prosper shook his head. "You'll need to ask *Madame* about that."

"She won't say it. She tells me nothing."

"Then I guess you've got your answer."

Vladimir stood there at the pen, helplessly, waiting for Prosper to offer a solution to his problem, but the man said nothing.

"What can we do?"

"You can do whatever you want to do. This isn't my trouble."

"That man is committing an act of infidelity against your own sister. You mean to say that this doesn't bother you?"

Prosper stopped and looked the Russian in the eye. "It is not my affair. If my sister comes to me and asks for help, I'll help. But not until then."

But his sister Josephina never did. Instead, late one bright afternoon, she swept the floor of her home, made a small and careful offering at an altar to one of her pagan gods, fed and watered the dogs, then hanged herself from a mangrove tree. So when Prosper came to me about it, I was much more eager to assist him than he'd been with me. He did not have a plan, he was far too blind with grief and rage to think anything through. But not I. I reasoned that the source of our misery was Honoré, therefore it would be necessary to put an end to that misery. My idea was so simple and logical, I never could have imagined it would end as it did...

The rain came in suddenly and violently, leaving Ana in a fearful state. Eulalie tried to calm her, but Ana knew this storm was not like the others. This was the storm that meant the red horse was coming, this time for real. She wanted to explain this to Eulalie, but knew it sounded like nonsense.

She'd heard her mother and father fighting in their bedroom, their angry voices echoing down the corridor, louder and far worse than the thunder and winds outside that rattled the house. Eulalie rocked her in her arms and tried in vain to distract the child, telling her stories about the far away place she was from, which sounded pretty enough, but Ana could only hear every few words, her attention focused on the chaos down the hall.

She heard a lot of bad words then, mostly from her father. He was calling her mother so many horrible names that Ana had not heard before. It was all so confusing, the way they screamed at each other in two different languages, and though Ana knew plenty of both, she still did not understand what some of the words meant. Eulalie spoke to her in quiet French, and between the three, after a while, Ana had no choice but to close her eyes and try to think of nothing, but this was impossible.

"There is a story in my mind," Ana said quietly, trying not to suck her thumb.

"Would you like to tell it to me?" Eulalie replied, and smoothed the child's hair.

"I will, but it is a bad story."

"Maybe if you tell me, it won't seem so bad afterwards."

Ana took a deep breath. "There was a lady, and she was very, very sad. She used to believe in God and spirits, but then she was so hurt that she could not believe in them anymore."

"That is very sad," Eulalie whispered. "What happened to her?"

"She went out to a tree and tied herself to a branch with a rope. Like this."

Ana put her hand to her throat and squeezed, and swayed back and forth in Eulalie's arms.

"Oh, child, no...no. Stop that now." Horrified, the woman blinked away tears, and held the child tight. "I do not wish to hear anymore of this story."

"No, but it's okay," Ana looked up at her with hopeful eyes. "Because when she was tying herself up there she was sad because she did not believe that God was real. But then when she fell down and was swinging, the last thing she knew was that he was."

After the longest time, it seemed, she heard quickened footsteps coming close. Eulalie rose and went to the door to see, as Veda rushed by, in tears. Vladimir followed a moment later, and Eulalie called after Veda, *"Madame! Don't go!"* but Veda did not stop, and it only prompted Vladimir to turn back and scream at her, too.

There were slamming doors, and then silence but for the storm outside.

When Eulalie turned around, Ana saw that there were tears in her eyes, but she quickly wiped them away and collected herself.

"It will be all right, *ma petite*. This storm, like the one out there, will blow over, too."

Ana knew it was true, but she knew things would not be the same once it did.

Honoré's wife was dead. *His wife was dead*, but still, he sat in the abandoned house where he and Veda had made love so many times, waiting for his mistress once again. They had not planned to meet on this night, but he hoped, despite the storm, she might hear his silent call and come.

He felt sick—not so much by the loss of Josephina, but by how little he felt. He reasoned that perhaps he was in shock, but beneath that, he knew it wasn't true. He hadn't loved Josephina for a very long time, and now there would be no denying it.

Surely, he had lost his soul to darkness, or worse—nothing. Perhaps he did not have a soul at all.

When he came home earlier that day she had not been in the house. He was relieved to not have to face her, for she'd gotten so much worse. He knew how she suffered from her unseen sickness, and that she would never recover, and he pitied her for it. But he could not take its constant presence in their home. It enshrouded her like a terrible black veil, blinding her and suffocating her until she could no longer function.

For years he'd tried to lift it from her, first delicately, and later, with sheer force, but it was sewn too tightly to her soul. He'd pleaded with the *loa* as he knew she had, but relief never seemed to come. At least not for her. But for him, it finally did. He knew his prayers had been heard the moment he saw Veda.

He'd poured himself a drink and sat at his table in relative peace, thinking about Veda. But his thoughts were soon disrupted by an ungodly cry from behind the house. He rushed to the window to see his brother-in-law standing beneath a tree, tearing at his hair and howling unintelligible words. The dogs were barking wildly, running in circles around the man, kicking up dirt and biting at each other, driven mad by the chaos around them. Honoré saw, but did not truly *see,* a familiar shape swaying through the air from a rope. *How odd,* he thought, not yet understanding the scene before him. It made no sense until the words that Prosper had been shrieking became clear.

"Josephina, *mon dieu*, Josephina!" Prosper cried, grasping at her legs, trying to still her, trying to save her.

But Honoré was paralyzed. He watched from the window as Prosper clumsily, desperately struggled with her legs, helpless to pull her down lest he tear her head from her body.

He knew he should've gone to him then, with tears in his eyes, and curses on his lips. He should have pulled his brother-in-law to the ground and let him scream until he'd purged himself, and then he should have helped him cut her down, but he did none of these things. Instead, he took a final heavy swig of his drink and quietly walked out the front door.

As he made his way to the abandoned cottage near the beach, the place where he and his answered prayer found humid, lustful comfort in each other, he noticed the storm in the distance. How suddenly the sky could change here. He knew it would soon be upon them.

What he did not know was that Prosper had seen the shadow of him slip away.

Ana wished her mother would come home; just walk through the door and run to her side. That was all she needed, that one simple thing. But Veda would not come home. She would weather the storm in the arms of a dark man. Ana saw this when she closed her eyes. She did not want to see them that way, but the pictures would not stop. She pushed her tiny hands against her eyes, trying to blur everything, but these were not like normal pictures. She saw this kind of picture on the inside of her eyes.

She saw it when another dark man came into the small, wooden house. She saw it when the two men argued terribly. She could not hear them, but she knew angry faces and angry hands. She saw her mother crying, and she saw it when the second man took a large knife from behind his back and drew it across the first man's throat. The red came in then, spraying and spilling over everything like her watercolours on paper. She pressed harder, but still the pictures did not stop. Then she saw her mother again. She was screaming now, cursing at the second man. The man paced around like a caged animal as the first man fell to his knees, still spraying from his neck. He clutched his throat as though he might stop it, but the blood still came. There was a wild look in his eye and he collapsed, his body jerking for a moment in an unnatural way before lying still. The second man stopped pacing and looked at Veda. She said something to him, and shook her head, though Ana could not hear her words. The man did not respond, but stood very still, surveying the scene. Then without warning, he lunged at her, grabbing her by the hair and pulling her toward him. Veda screamed and screamed and Ana watched, helplessly trapped in her vision, as the man forced her beautiful mother to her knees and drew the knife across her throat, too.

After that, she could not scream anymore.

The whole world had gone red. And then she saw that the man was not a man at all, but a red horse, wild and mad. He grunted and screamed and howled and drove his knife into the splintered, bloodstained floor, then ran away into the darkness, slick and red. When Ana opened her eyes, he was gone. Everything was gone.

She did not cry then, nor did she wholly understand what she had seen, but she knew, as she stared into the darkness of her room, listening to the rain and the wind beat itself mercilessly against the house, it meant that she would never see her mother again.

⤳

Étienne spared no expense on the arrangements for Veda and she was buried in a small mausoleum at the Grégoire family plot, at his insistence. Vladimir acquiesced to this, but refused to allow the members of the town's *Société*, with their hedonism and black magic, to attend the small but lavish funeral. He did not know that Étienne let them come under the cover of night to pay their respects and say farewell to their *Madame*.

Honoré was buried in a simple plot on a hillside, next to Josephina.

Martine, poised to leave the estate, was persuaded to stay when she saw that Eulalie was likely to become Ana's sole caretaker. She said only that she could not leave her sister to care for the entire household alone.

Prosper was gone, as though he'd disappeared into the darkness and stayed there, even after the sun came up. The sisters never saw their cousin again.

It was days before Ana spoke to anyone. Her father spent his time the way he had before, acting strangely and sleeping all the time, though some nights she thought she could hear him weeping. In waking hours, she noticed that he could barely bring himself to look at her.

Eulalie found the terrible china doll in the garden the morning of the funeral and without a word to anyone, burned it in a small pit down by the goats. It burned easily and quickly turned to ash, something that Eulalie knew would not have happened before. She made no mention of it afterwards to Ana, knowing that the child would be relieved to forget, if given the chance. She hoped she'd never ask.

And she never did.

But while Ana did not make mention of the doll, her nightmare was not over. She could still see the pictures, and now, amidst the weeping of her father and the sisters, she could hear her mother's voice in everything. It was comforting at first, but she soon longed for everyone to just be quiet.

It was peaceful at her mother's grave. She thought Veda's voice might be louder there, but it wasn't, and she was grateful. It was lovely there at the edge of the plantation, with orchids and chalky white stone chambers and crosses, and lush, green ferns. Ana thought it looked more like a fairyland than a cemetery and decided that it would be her new secret, quiet place. She only wished she could have spent as much time with her mother while she was still alive.

The clay jar appeared at Veda's grave seven days after the burial. It was small and the colour of an ashen plum, with a tiny, jagged white cross etched on the side. It was also empty, as far as Ana could tell. She'd come to the grave each day and had never before seen the jar, yet she knew that it was meant to be hers.

When her father saw the mysterious gift, he told her he did not approve of her having it and took it away, but the next day, she woke to see the jar at her bedside. She kept it close to her all day, and Martine asked her all about it, so she told her what she knew. Martine said she'd been right to take it. It belonged to her.

But when her father saw her with the jar a second time, he took it from her again and scolded her for disobeying. She did not understand, she thought he'd given it back to her, and she was scolded yet again for fibbing.

The following day, she was careful to hide the jar, which had, once again, appeared at her bedside. She managed to keep it from her father's sight for another whole day before he saw it.

This time, he was furious. He snatched the jar from her tiny hands and shook it at her as he yelled. She wanted to cry but would not do such a thing in front of him. She decided then and there that she would never again act like a baby in his presence. Her mother was gone and she knew that she did not trust this man to care for her. She would need to care for herself from then on.

He continued to yell at her, and she continued to keep her tears at bay, even when he smashed the jar on the floor.

Martine and Eulalie burst in at the commotion and collectively gasped at the sight of the broken jar. Still, Ana held back the tears, but Eulalie could see the desperation on the child's face.

"Do not fret, *ma petite*. This belongs to you and it always will," Eulalie whispered, sadly, as she and her sister picked up the pieces. Eulalie knew it was true, even though she didn't want it to be.

⤴

When Vladimir saw his daughter the next day with the jar, intact and without fractures as though it had never been broken, he felt sick with the knowledge that something sinister had befallen them. This was revenge, the kind of revenge he'd experienced once before with Ivo, and he knew that he was no longer safe from ghosts. No matter where he went, or what he did, they would come.

Nearly paralysed by the crushing weight of his guilt and his grief and fear, he could not bring himself to visit Veda's grave. He could not even close his eyes at night without seeing her in her coffin; her beautiful, young face, no longer olive-hued but pale, and seeming paler still beneath her silken black hair, her delicate hands resting on her still heart, and an ornate choker of lace and shells about her neck —her perfect swan neck— to cover the killing wound. That would be the last and most prominent image of her he would ever have. He drank heavily, trying to wash away the vision of her and fall into some semblance of guiltless sleep, but it had been at his suggestion that she now lay in a cold crypt while the world went on without her, and there would be no sanctuary for him anywhere. Not in sleep, and not in death.

⤴

They could not stay in Martinique much longer. The people there knew that even though Prosper had committed the murders with his own hands, they'd been guided, in part, by another's, and the Russian's motive was as clear as the sea. He was hated now, by the *Société*, by the sisters, by the plantation workers, and would, before long, be hated by his own child. His only remaining ally was Étienne, who was too much of a gentleman to make such accusations and too much of an addict to give it any deeper thought.

Étienne gave Vladimir the name of a former colleague in London and helped him secure passage for himself and the child. Ana would be placed in a girls' school in Staffordshire, far away from Vladimir and his misery. He said it was so she could have a stable and proper rearing, but in truth, he simply could not bear to forever see Veda in her dark eyes, looking upon him with hatred and betrayal.

"Do you know why this is so special?" Martine asked Ana of her jar.

Ana shook her head no.

"It is special because it holds your *mama's esprit.*"

Ana's eyes widened. "It feels like Mama."

"We wanted her to be with you. To keep you safe, and so you will never be alone."

Eulalie sat quietly with her sewing, keeping her head down.

"So you keep that near to your heart, *ma petite.*"

Ana nodded obediently and wandered away, clutching the little clay jar.

"*We* didn't want that, Martine. You and your people wanted that. Not I," Eulalie said.

"She never should have lost her mother. This is the least we can give her," Martine replied. "And *my people* are *your people*, too, sister. Like it or not."

"That child is going to have enough torment without a ghost following her around. So what of that?"

"It is the right thing, Eula."

"For whom, Martine? You? The *Société*? For Ana's heart? Veda's revenge? Do not be so quick, sister, to think you can know the grand design for that child.

You haven't seen what I seen in her, and you're messing with things you ought not be messing with."

"That awful man is going to take her from us. Who will protect her then?" Martine whispered sharply.

"The same one that protects us all. God."

London 1887

Pinkney was amused by his strange, new friend. The man seemed so lost, yet so determined, and Pinkney was having a grand time unravelling his mystery.

The stranger fiddled with the pendant—a small wooden cross—at his neck and stared intently at his glass. Pinkney tried to think of words the stranger might know, but was met only with looks of confusion and frustration. After several futile exchanges, the man reached into his coat and showed Pinkney a photograph.

Pinkney's eyes lit up at once. It was too good to be true.

"This man," the stranger said.

Pinkney smiled and nodded. "Oh, my yes," he laughed to himself. "*That* man. Yes, mate, yes. You come to the right place!"

The end was coming. This much Vladimir knew for certain. But in regards to everything else, he was certain of nothing. He could no longer trust his senses after such consistent betrayal. He did not know who was real, and who was a figment of his imagination, who was alive and who was dead. At times, he wondered if he was the one who had died, and this pale existence was his hell. Sometimes he could smell Constanta or Martinique, and other times all he could smell was the human pollution of the city. Sometimes, he could hear Veda's voice drifting through the hall, or in through the window, and sometimes he could hear nothing but the arrhythmic beating of his sick, guilty heart. But the end was coming, indeed, and soon his senses and his suffering would cease to matter.

≈

I know my word means nothing to you, but please believe me when I tell you that taking you from Martinique and sending you away to school was the hardest thing I ever had to do. But making sure you were far away from my cursed soul was the only right *thing I could do for you.*

≈

Vladimir left much behind in Martinique: his research, his books, myriad personal belongings, the body of his wife, and a broken-hearted Étienne. The Frenchman and the sisters had all but begged him to leave the child behind; they would raise her well and she would never want for anything, but Vladimir would not hear of it. He could scarcely believe the audacity of the two women to suggest such a thing. He could only imagine what would become of Ana if left to those uneducated heathens, and felt that his soul could not stand to bear any more marks against it, so he took his money and his daughter and went to England where he was unknown.

Where he was not a murderer.

But when he left Martinique and the sanctuary that was the Grégoire Plantation, he exposed himself and his child to all the vengeful ghosts he'd left behind, and to the one that would follow them from the island.

London 1875

Once Ana was safely tucked away at the boarding school in Staffordshire, Vladimir set about finding a flat in London. He did not know the city, nor did he care to try. He only wanted a room in which to sit quietly and clear his mind. His soul, he knew, was beyond salvation.

He found that room, above a pub, right by the river. He did not remember the name of the innkeeper that rented him the flat, nor did he know the name of the neighbourhood, or even recognize his own neighbours. He was ready to be a ghost, anonymous and silent, so that was what he became.

He drank alone in his one-room flat most nights, staring at the gaslight on the grey, chipped wall until it became a blur, and he would fade away, each time, hoping it would be the last.

~≋~

He met Lloyd Pinkney the following December during one of his rare visits to the downstairs pub. Upon first glance, he thought the small, pallid man was suffering from the dreadful cold, but when he failed to regain his colour after two shots of whiskey, Vladimir realised he was just unusually pale. If only he hadn't been staring with tepid curiosity, perhaps he could've avoided ever meeting Pinkney. But he was, and he did, and there wasn't much to be done about it after the fact.

Pinkney referred to himself as a business manager, but in reality, he was nothing more than a pimp. Vladimir despised him from the moment the man opened his mouth; he was merely a lower class version of Vladimir's father. At least Viktor had educated his girls, and demanded they meet the highest of standards. Pinkney, on the other hand, preyed on the destitute and the young, and this made Vladimir sick to his core.

But it wasn't long until Vladimir found himself soliciting Pinkney's services. He was only human, after all, and he was quick to insist that Pinkney not send him anyone who was too young. He was also quick to remark that this interaction did not make he and Pinkney friends. Their dealings would be of a professional nature only.

Vladimir *did* eventually make a friend, or at least an acquaintance whom he could trust. William Grace was an accountant, and a close friend of the inn-keeper whose name Vladimir could never remember. His visits to the pub had become more frequent, as did his dealings with Pinkney, which was not at all a coincidence, and Vladimir was pleased to have, in that time, met someone who was the exact opposite of Pinkney.

Grace was an intelligent and soft-spoken man. He came from a successful family—both his brother and father were attorneys—but he refused to live on his family's money. He made his own way, which afforded him a very modest life, and Vladimir admired and envied this greatly, for he had once tried and failed to do the same. Grace also had a child—a son—a few years older than Ana. He was called Nicholas, and Vladimir thought that Nicholas Grace sounded like a fine and honest man's name.

Vladimir saw a glimmer of what he could have been in William, and this saddened him, though the mere presence of a decent soul in his life illuminated his cold and darkened heart, even if in the smallest way.

But the single kindest thing William ever did for Vladimir was to take care of the Russian's finances without asking too many questions. In fact, William never asked Vladimir too many questions about anything, and Vladimir was quite content with that.

Pinkney, however, rarely stopped asking questions. He was eternally pry-ing into Vladimir's past, and the drunker Vladimir got, the more he would divulge. As a result, Pinkney knew far too much, and he used the information to his advantage at every possible turn, making him a kind of necessary evil in Vladimir's already damned existence.

And then there was the matter of Ivo.

He visited his murderer nightly for the longest time, sometimes showing up in the pub or following him in the streets, other times invading the flat and staying until he was sated. There were no talismans for Vladimir, no chemistry to protect him. He would be forced to live with whatever demons came.

If Ivo had been cruel in life, he was even more venomous in death. Vladimir had no secrets from Ivo. The wraith knew every terrible thing that Vladimir had ever thought or done, and he wasted no time torturing him for his crimes.

He drove himself into Vladimir's nightmares, making him dream of Veda. Veda in her casket, Veda drowning in the Black Sea, Veda losing the pearls Étienne had given to her into the open gash in her neck. Strangers—and sometimes Ivo, himself— in a lavish parlour taking turns performing sickening, lustful acts with the wound. Sometimes she would become his mother, split into pieces, her tiny bones falling to the floor. And sometimes he wielded the knife that slit his wife open. He knew this was Ivo's doing because only a diabolical soul could summon such horrendous images. Veda, even with a vengeful heart, could never be so ugly.

❧

All the while, you were becoming such a proper young lady. Do you remember that, for a time, you would write me letters? You'd tell me what you were learning in school, and sometimes you'd confess small, secret things to me, like the time you took your mother's string of pearls to wear, but lost them while playing with the goats. She wondered what had become of them, but believed she had merely misplaced them. She would not have been angry with you, had she known. She always cared more about love and emotion than tangible objects. It pains me to think of the things you've carried with you, and I hope in revealing them to me, you found some solace. Perhaps the Sisters there were prompting you to do so, or perhaps you just wished to let go of certain things. Either way, I was not ~am not, still~ worthy of your confessions, and that you ever shared any secret with me at all brought me more joy than I could ever say. I've saved every single letter.

❧

"This is too good. This is jus' too good," Pinkney said with a tear of joy in his eye. "I wonder what sort of trouble our dear Mille'ovo has got his'self into that someone would come so far to find 'im. I can only imagine!"

Luca stared at the man, not understanding why he was so gleeful.

"Aw, mate...you ain' got a clue as to what I'm sayin', but that's quite all right. We're gonna drink our drinks, then I'm gonna take you right to our friend here," he gestured to the tattered photograph. "Can't help you with his lovely friend, though. I'd seen 'er, I'd surely remember." He smiled, showing his little rat teeth.

Luca nodded slowly. "Yes. This man. Vladimir...Millerovo."

Then Pinkney saw something in the stranger's face. Some odd, tight lines around his mouth; a severity in his black eyes, an almost imperceptible trembling beneath his dark skin. It was in that sobering moment that the pub became like some icy, silent cave; the air around them thin and sharp, and Pinkney no longer felt like laughing.

"A'ight, mate," he said cautiously. "You wait 'ere. You understand? Wait. 'ere." He made a motion with his hand as though Luca were a dog he was commanding to stay, and hurried, nervously, for the door.

❧

Vladimir had grown weary of his story. There was so much ugliness in the pages before him and he wondered how he'd ever find the courage to see it reach Ana. He hoped with sincerity—not self-pity—that he would be dead by the time she received it.

And—dear god—the knocking. He was so weary of that as well. Maybe it was Ivo, come for his nightly tormenting. Vladimir reasoned that he needn't bother to answer the door; Ivo would find his way in, regardless. He always did.

But it did not cease, and finally Vladimir could not hear any more of it.

He was disgusted to find a breathless Pinkney on the other side.

"What?" he snapped, rubbing his stubbled face. "What do you want from me?"

Pinkney cast his eyes to the floor and caught his breath. "Can I come in?"

This was not the Lloyd Pinkney that Vladimir knew; this meek, humbled man in his doorway. He would have never invited the other Lloyd Pinkney in.

"Are you going to tell me what this is about?"

"There's…there's a man. Downstairs. 'e ain' from around 'ere."

"And?" Vladimir sat down at his table, rubbed his unshaven face furiously and stared blankly at the journal.

"And… 'e's lookin' for you. 'e's even got his'self a picture of you."

Vladimir breathed in deeply. His hands began to shake. "What picture?"

"Ah, i's a photograph of you an' a woman. A really beautiful woman. With black 'air." Beads of sweat slowly formed on Pinkney's forehead.

"Tell me, does the man also have black hair? Does he look like the woman?" Suddenly, he felt like crying.

"He does. But…ah, I think…"

Vladimir looked him in the eyes without malice, possibly for the first time since they'd met.

"…I think 'e means to 'arm you…"

Vladimir nodded slowly, knowingly.

"…in the worst sense of the word. I don' know it for certain, but…I do. I s'pose that don' make much sense, now…" Pinkney turned his eyes to the floor once more. "'e's got me bloody spooked!"

"No. It makes all the sense in the world."

"What're we gonna do?"

Vladimir smiled in spite of himself as a few tears fell. Suddenly he and Pinkney were '*we*'. He was slightly touched.

"Does he know that I'm here?"

Pinkney shook his head quickly. "No. Well, yes. But I did'n say where, exactly. I was gonna tell 'im…up until I seen 'e—what 'e meant to do, that is."

"Then I need you to do me a favour. Well, another favour, I suppose I should say."

Pinkney nodded.

"Go to him and tell him that you will bring him to me tomorrow night. Say '*mâine noapte.*' He will understand. But please do not bring him here any sooner. Can you do this for me?"

Pinkney repeated the words quietly three times then said, "Aye. But what are you gonna do?"

"I'm going to finish what I started."

⤜

As you read these words ~if you have come this far~ time will have moved differently for you than it has for me. I do not know if, for you, it is night or day, if it is summer or winter. It could be any Wednesday or it could be Christmas. The only thing I am certain of is where I am at in this very moment, as I write these words, and that is London, in my flat, on the second-to-last day of my life.

⤜

It was, as Vladimir expected, a long and torturous night. But he would finish the journal, no matter. Even if Ivo came.

Or Mary.

Or Katya.

Or—god help him—Veda.

Were they not all the same now? Were they not merely the natural consequences of a guilty heart?

"Oh, why not, my tragic friends?" he called out to the empty room. "Will you all deny me one last hurrah before I join you?"

He took a hefty swig from the bottle of absinthe he'd been nursing since the morning. The taste of anise burned and cooled his throat at the same time.

"Where are you? Where are you, my dead whores? My dearest friend? And Veda? Oh, god, Veda," he sobbed and threw the bottle at the wall, smashing it into a hundred glistening pieces.

"*No!* No, I have work to do," he said to no one and wiped his face violently. "None of you are more important than that. She is the only thing that matters now. She's the only thing that ever mattered."

No one came, and he went back to the journal.

It has come to this, my darling heart~ the end. The end of my ~our~ story, and the end of me. But it is not the end for you. I have done what I could to ensure you the things I could not give you when you were a child ~stability, a home, a family that will care for you, and this. The truth found in these pages is something I have owed you for a very long time, and I'm sorry that I was never strong enough to tell you in person. I find myself feeling grateful that my time here is almost over, because I know that due to my cowardice and folly you would never again have me in your life, and I would rather be dead than live another day without you.

I do not know how to do this, how to write the proper final words. I have set arrangements for you, so ~if you choose~ you will be taken care of for the rest of your life, but do not mistake my intentions. Truly, I have no right to give you advice on how to live your life. I have no right to anything. All I can say is that I know you will carry on in spite of the pain I have inflicted upon you, and you will be glorious, no matter what you choose. And I know that the last image I will bring to mind, before it is dark, will be one of you and your mother, laughing beneath a wall of bougainvillea, on a beautiful island, surrounded by the bluest sea, in a rare and precious moment of serenity. A brief moment when we were nothing but love.

Eternally yours,
Papa

Death came knocking, as he knew it would, the next night. It did not pound angrily, it did not raise its voice. It just came knocking, the way any gentleman would.

Vladimir let it in.

Luca stood before him, a bag slung over one shoulder, still perfect, still the near mirror image of his sister—a sight that chilled Vladimir to his very core. He offered his brother-in-law a chair, and took the seat across from him.

When he spoke to Luca, it was in his native tongue.

"I knew one day you'd come."

"Did you?"

"We both knew. You knew long before I."

"Yes."

"Iona was right about me."

"She was right about most things."

"Was? Has she passed?"

"The news of my sister's death stilled her heart. But don't worry. She will be waiting for you on the other side."

Vladimir smiled slightly, grimly.

"I know why you're here."

Luca leaned forward, close to Vladimir and whispered, "How should we do it, I have wondered?"

Vladimir was silent.

"We could slit your throat so you could feel what my sister felt as her life drained away," Luca continued. "Or I could beat you to death. Or maybe we could drown you in the river."

Still, Vladimir said nothing.

"But then I decided I would rather watch you take your own life, for unlike you, I am not a murderer."

"If you are not willing to become a murderer, how do you intend to force my hand?"

"There is no forcing here. You and I will talk. And when that is done, I will leave you to die."

"It sounds so simple."

"It is."

"I would offer you a drink, but," he motioned to the broken glass on floor, "I have nothing left to give."

"You never did. But no matter. I've brought us a gift," Luca said as he pulled a bottle of vodka from his bag.

"My favourite."

"Glasses?"

Vladimir retrieved two glasses from a small wooden shelf and placed them on the table.

Luca poured.

Neither drank.

"I thought you weren't a murderer, Luca?"

"Have I poured it down your throat?"

"No."

They were silent for a moment, looking at their glasses, then each other.

"I understand why you would pour a glass for me, but why for yourself?"

Luca sighed. "Do you understand nothing I've ever said to you? My sister was my other half. It was difficult enough living without her before, but at least I had the comfort of knowing she was in this world. Then you murdered her, and

185

the other half of me was gone. Irreversibly. Permanently. I cannot go through the rest of my life this way."

"I never meant for her to be hurt, Luca. You must know that. She wasn't supposed to be there," he closed his eyes and gasped for air, gasped for the words. "She should never have been there."

"So it was her fault? Is that what you mean to say, you gutless monster?"

"No. I pushed her there. I pushed her to him and I pushed her to her death."

"Do you know that I felt it when she died? Before that cursed letter ever came to us, I felt it. I felt her fear, her confusion. Do you know that she did not understand what was happening at first? She did not understand why the room darkened and spun, nor why her dress had become wet; why she could not speak. She saw the knife. She saw what became of the other man, yet when it was her turn, nothing made sense, as though when that blade slit her throat, it severed her reasoning. But it did not sever mine."

Luca lit a cigarette and let it burn.

"Do you know that she did not understand that the blood that sprayed across the room was coming from her?"

Tears fell hard and fast from Vladimir's eyes into his mouth and onto the table, but Luca did not relent.

"Finally, when she was empty, her blood gone, when it had painted the entire room in red, she still felt…" Luca choked back his own tears "…she felt cold and afraid. So afraid. But it was not for herself. She felt afraid for you and Anastacia because she knew she was leaving you and there was nothing she could do. And that fear…that was the very last thing she ever felt."

"I'm so sorry…I'm…" Vladimir said. He turned his eyes to the ceiling, fearfully, as though god might break through and burn him to cinders with his touch.

"But it does not end there," Luca continued. "I feel her in the wind, in the rain, in every storm, but I do not feel her in me. Not anymore. You stole that from me. You stole that from your daughter. But my sister will haunt us

186

all, as long as we breathe. She cannot be at peace because that is not what surrounded her when she died. She is a terrible storm. She is chaos. And she will be vengeance. This is how you've left my magnificent sister—as a *wraith*. As a raging open wound, and I *cannot* curse you enough. Hell does not go as deep as you deserve."

Vladimir closed his eyes and grieved. For the first time, he truly grieved.

There were no more words. The night faded into a grey dawn and the cigarettes burned away, but there were no more words.

At last, when the gaslight burned out, Vladimir drank.

It tasted like home, for better or for worse.

He looked to Luca to take his turn, but he only laughed and said, "Did you truly believe I would follow you into death? Or hold your hand? Did you really think I would accompany you—*you*—when my sister had to go alone? It has always been *your world*, hasn't it? You were an island that she was so graciously allowed to swim near, but never to thrive upon. It was always your needs, your desires, your pain, your fear. *Poor Dimi, how tortured he has been—a kitten amidst the hungry wolves.*"

Vladimir raised his head, his eyes were wild. "How did you…?"

But Luca did not acknowledge his confusion.

"No, Vladimir, you will go to death alone and afraid, just like you forced her to do. The world will cease to revolve around you, and you will be what you always truly were—*nothing*."

He emptied his glass onto the floor, picked up his bag, and walked toward the door.

"What of your missing half, Luca? What of *your* end?" Vladimir whispered.

Luca turned to face his sister's killer one last time and said, "I'm already dead. I died with her."

Then he was gone, and there was nothing more for Vladimir to do but to wait for death to claim him.

He remembered the bougainvillea.

Epilogue

Lancashire 1887

Ana watched nervously as the workers hauled cart after cart of slate from the pit that lay deeper into the woods. She held tightly to her little clay jar as she watched, tracing the rim with her finger, over and over again. It was here. She could smell it in the trails of slate dust the men were leaving behind their carts, like a wolf smells the blood trail of its wounded prey. She needed to go to the woods. That's where it lived—in the woods. She hoped she was ready. Nicholas had been so kind, building her this exquisite home. She hadn't the heart to tell him that her only true home was someplace dark, someplace cold. She knew this in her damaged soul because she'd seen it a hundred times in dreams. She knew he'd never understand. No one would ever understand.

Her heart pounded in her throat and her stomach fluttered violently. It was too much—her mother's voice, her father's journal, the marriage and the house—everything. If she'd had one wish, it would have been to be free of them all.

"It's going to be remarkable, don't you think?" Nicholas said as he approached his young bride, his smooth, pale face flushed with the colour of excitement like a little boy at Christmas.

She gazed upon the frame of the great house. "It looks like bones," she said thoughtfully. "Like the bones of an ancient creature that would have devoured us if given the chance."

But Nicholas only laughed. "Missus Grace, you have quite the imagination! The things you say!"

He kissed her on the forehead and smiled. "What would make you happiest right at this moment?"

"I think I might like to go for a walk," she said softly.

"Shall I escort you?"

"No, my love. You stay here and make sure no one gets eaten." She attempted a smile of her own. She hoped he did not see her tremble as she walked away.

At the far edge of the woods the sounds of the workers echoed through the trees, their voices distant and hollow.

She could feel the quarry before she could see it; she could feel its massive presence, a great beast lying still. Breathing shallow. Waiting.

The trees gave way then and she saw it. It was magnificent. The ground had been opened like an awful, ancient mouth before her, a mouth filled with men, filled with lies, filled with secrets, and she knew she was home. She'd waited her whole life to find this awesome, terrible sanctuary. It was the one place in the world that could house her fear and rage.

She laughed when she threw the clay jar that held her mother's soul into that mouth, knowing it would not come back to her, as it had done so many times when she was a child. When it shattered, it barely made a sound.

Had it been up to her, she would have thrown all of them in with it: her father, Ivo, her father's dead whores, Honoré, Prosper and that terrible blood-horse. With its jagged walls and cold, isolated darkness, the quarry would have made the perfect home for the lot of them. But now it would only belonged to the two of them, Veda and Ana. She would protect it the way she'd wished someone would have protected her, and in the quarry she would have the mother she'd always longed for. Here, her mother could thrive.

She watched as the workers tore shards from her walls and took them to the house. It was painful, but things would be as they needed to be. It was the only way for the quarry to spread her arms beyond the woods.

"Don't worry," down on hands and knees, she whispered to the pit. "I'll see you get everything you need."

She pressed her mouth to a cold piece of slate that jutted out from the quarry's edge, and smiled. There were so many men, down inside of her, working—not knowing what they were creating. Ana pitied them for a moment, but remembered how deep and cold the hearts and minds of men could be. Her new mother had been starving for so long, waiting for her with a dry and dusty mouth. These men would be the first of many to sate her.

In the journal, her father said her story had not ended. He did not know how right he was. And if she could have, she would have thanked him for leading her here. It was the only thing she would ever love him for. But his own terrible horse had already come and carried him away, and there would be no telling him now.

She stared into the depths of the quarry—her new, cold mother—knowing how long it had been waiting for her and the soul she'd brought with her. She felt her heart beating strong for the first time since she was a little girl, and she smiled. Truly, there would be so much more hell to come, she thought. There was still *so* much to do, but it was fine. The thing she'd waited for her entire life had finally happened.

She was home.

About the Author

Donna Lynch is a dark fiction writer and the co-founder—along with her husband, artist and musician Steven Archer—of the dark electro-rock band Ego Likeness (Metropolis Records). Her written works include *Isabel Burning*, *Driving Through the Desert*, *Ladies & Other Vicious Creatures*, *Daughters of Lilith*, and *In My Mouth*. She and her husband live in Maryland.

CPSIA information can be obtained at www.ICGtesting.com
Printed in the USA
BVOW07s0155220713

326133BV00002B/8/P